The Reunion
A Novel

RAJ VELAMOOR

 FriesenPress

Suite 300 - 990 Fort St
Victoria, BC, V8V 3K2
Canada

www.friesenpress.com

Copyright © 2021 by Raj Velamoor
First Edition — 2021

All rights reserved.

No part of this publication may be reproduced in any form, or by any means, electronic or mechanical, including photocopying, recording, or any information browsing, storage, or retrieval system, without permission in writing from FriesenPress.

ISBN
978-1-03-911836-2 (Hardcover)
978-1-03-911835-5 (Paperback)
978-1-03-911837-9 (eBook)

1. FICTION, LITERARY

Distributed to the trade by The Ingram Book Company

TABLE OF CONTENTS

Testimonials	v
Dedication	ix
A Word of Thanks	xi
Preface	xiii
The Families	xvii
Chapter 1	1
Chapter 2	11
Chapter 3	23
Chapter 4	35
Chapter 5	47
Chapter 6	55
Chapter 7	69
Chapter 8	77
Chapter 9	85
Chapter 10	95
Chapter 11	105
Chapter 12	113
Chapter 13	123
Chapter 14	139
Chapter 15	149
Chapter 16	209
Epilogue	217
Glossary of Indian Terms	227
Acknowledgements	233
About the Author	235

TESTIMONIALS

I fancy myself an honorary member of the 21 million strong Indian Diaspora. I have this in mind as I turn to review this Novel, The Reunion. The Reunion, after a 55 years lapse, takes place over a weekend in Vir's 6-bedroom house in Michigan. Patel, the Jeweler, worries if he would fit in with the group now comprised of 3 Doctors, and two engineers. The "Doctor thing" is an undercurrent in this novel. When a Character is asked "How is your Son?" he replies: "He is a doctor. Doing well" . The author sets his novel against the major currents of world affairs of the last 5 decades and the Reunion chatter covers sexual abuse, homosexuality, immigration, race, caste, and politics. The two US based characters are living the "American Dream" and are supporters of the 2020 Defeated Republican Presidential candidate. Despite some uneasiness among the Group, they seem to be having a jolly good time. Then it is all spoilt by a traumatic event. As I read the stories of the 5 who left India, l wonder whether migration is a cultural rupture and immigrants are doomed to live lives of mimicry. Vas, the one who remained in Hyderabad and who tried to convince the White Police Officer in Michigan that he had a Driver in India appears chastened on his return but was comforted by returning "home". The author's description of the history of the city of Hyderabad, the culture, the family dynamics is well written and reflect a personal pride of place that lives in his characters. It is a humane and serious novel.

> Emmanuel Persad. Professor Emeritus, Western University, Ontario. Canada.

*****

In this lovely, intriguing, and psychologically astute novel, noted psychiatrist Varadaraj Velamoor crafts a heartfelt tale of six friends whose relationship bridges continents, cultures, and centuries. His finely-crafted novel shines when it describes the life - both internal and external - of the generation of educated Indians who grew up in post-Independence India, many of whom spread across the world to enrich and transform the nations they came to inhabit.

> Gautam Mukunda, Research Fellow, Harvard Kennedy School, Author of "Indispensable: When Leaders Really Matter and Picking Presidents: How To Make The Most Important Decision in the World", Host, Nasdaq's World Reimagined with Gautam Mukunda.

*****

In "The Reunion", Dr. Velamoor brings a motley cast of characters from diverse backgrounds to life, with differences in caste, religion, language and social standing. In doing so, he takes us, the readers, on a journey through time and place, as we read about judges in Hyderabad, jewelers in Birmingham and doctors in the US and Canada. He also deftly weaves in narratives about historical events from the 1960s to the present both in India as well as in all the western countries where most of the protagonists live. This book also takes the readers through a rollercoaster of emotions – I experienced nostalgia for an India that does not exist anymore, admiration for countries that accept immigrants for their skills and contributions without caring about what they look like, pride at a Canada that has made multiculturalism more than just a buzzword, and anger at how some immigrants forget where they really are from in their efforts to blend in. My only complaint about this book is a good sort of complaint, I wish it was longer.

> Partha Mohanram is a chaired professor at the University of Toronto, having taught at Columbia and NYU before. He obtained his PhD from Harvard and was educated at India's elite engineering (IIT-Madras) and management (IIM-Ahmedabad) institutes prior to that. This book was particularly appealing to him, as he grew up in a very similar multi-ethnic and multi-religious diverse environment in Mumbai.

*****

The Reunion begins with six boys growing up in Hyderabad, a southern city in India, and Velamoor affectionately weaves a compelling tale of their lives in the larger context of post-independence India. The backdrop is the cauldron of caste, class and religion; as well as the urge to seek fame and fortune in the West. All six men essentially join the hard working and successful "model minority" while their strong links to each other and to India are dramatically weakened. At the point when they reach their retirement age on three continents, they reconnect after fifty years and plan a reunion in Michigan. Their encounter reveals certain deep differences that once again reflect class and religious differences and, when confronted with Trump's America, race becomes a factor in this heady mix. This debut novel will resonate well with the South Asian diaspora as it holds up a mirror to this sizeable population in so many ways.

Manjunath Pendakur immigrated to Canada in 1969 and earned a Ph.D. in communications, specializing in the political economy of the media. He became professor and chair of the Department of Radio-TV-Film at Northwestern University in Chicago where he taught for18 years. He also served as Dean at three public universities. His scholarly publications include a number of books and journal articles on the global media industry, including a book on Canadian cinema and a book on Indian cinema.

DEDICATION

Dear Amiya, Sahil, Dhara, and Milin,

Stories are important to tell. We learn how to live by listening to them. This is a story of people who come from the same place as I have.

Your story is important, as there is no one in the world like you.

I dedicate this to you and your parents. You are everything to me.

With much love,
Banka

A WORD OF THANKS

From Hyderabad I am
The city of forts and dams
Where the culture of north
Mingles with the south
Where pearls are strung
And church bells rung
Where tongues many spoken
And barriers of religion broken
Where the muezzin call
Echoes through temple halls
Where bridges are built
And friendships forged and sealed
I am who I am
As from Hyderabad I am

PREFACE

This book was not meant to be. It had never occurred to me that I could write a book of fiction. I have published some scientific papers and dabbled recently in amateur poetry writing. But writing a novel was a bridge too far. Upon my retirement from active practise in 2016, a colleague of mine presented me with a notebook encased in a soft, brown, leather jacket. He said I could use it to jot things down. It was the size of a short novel. That was the first time the thought crossed my mind. A passing thought at best.

A few years passed, and then the COVID-19 pandemic hit us. Like millions, I too felt isolated and confined with time hanging heavily. I picked up the notebook one day and placed it by my bedside. And then one morning, I began to write. I let my thoughts flow as they came. A stream of consciousness, if you like, to see where it would take me. It was like laying bricks randomly without a blueprint, not knowing what the edifice would look like. It did not matter at the time, as I was writing for my own pleasure. I let the plot form and characters emerge as they pleased.

Growing up in my home in India, I was in awe of the library of books displayed in two steel cabinets. The "Indian

Council of World Affairs," a think-tank to study international affairs, appointed my father, a university professor in political science, as the custodian of the collection. He ran it like a library. His faculty colleagues borrowed books and returned them as they might from a library. My father maintained a ledger as a librarian would. There were books on world wars by Churchill, history of the world by Toynbee, biographies of Jawaharlal Nehru and Mahatma Gandhi, and political philosophies of Marx and Engels, Kant, Locke, and Hobbes, and much more. I leafed through them casually, extracting passages now and then to insert in my presentations at school and college contests. However, there was not much fiction or literature in the collection. I wonder now how he managed to read the classics and works of literature and quote passages from memory. He could not have afforded to buy books, having come from a family of meagre means. He must have borrowed them from school and public libraries. He was a fount of knowledge, and his clever use and play on words is part of the family folklore. Like my siblings and cousins, I was influenced to write and speak like him. Sadly, with digitization of books and online reading, libraries which were hitherto hubs of learning are now under siege. One doesn't go to a library anymore. It comes to us. But only if we have broadband connectivity.

It was not until I married my wife, Suha, in my late twenties that I developed an interest in fiction. Over the years, she has bought hundreds of books by various authors from different lands to make a decent compilation. The books have travelled with us from country to country. I have come to admire writers like R.K. Narayan of India,

Coetzee of South Africa, McEwan of England, and Alice Munro of Canada. They have the ability to weave a good story in no more than two hundred pages, by not using ten words if five would do, as my father often advised.

Another impetus to write came later. A few years ago, I emailed a couple of friends in our condo building in Toronto to ask if they were interested in starting a book club. We now have one. It consists of ten accomplished people from different walks of life. Each one interprets a book through a unique lens bringing their personal life experiences to bear on the review. I have come to know some of them well and the "worlds" they live in.

The morning cup of coffee was the stimulant that fired my seventy-five-year-old brain. I wrote daily for three to four hours lounging in my bed. I highly recommend this form of levity. In times like this, it is good for the soul. This novel, as I said, evolved from a "no holds barred" version initially to several subsequent drafts as I revised and refined it. I am grateful to my wife for her help throughout this process. She is an avid reader and has an uncanny ability to analyze. She finds angles and nuances that others have missed.

I have drawn from some historical events that touched the city of Hyderabad, my hometown in India. I was raised in a melting pot of cultures. These were seminal events that influenced relations between residents of different castes and religions. The tussle between innate traits and environmental influences is reflected in the lives of the characters.

Their role in the interplay of politics between nations even separated by oceans is intriguing.

The characters in the book are fictional. They are figments of my imagination. Any resemblance to anyone is fortuitous. If I have offended any sensitivities or sensibilities, it was unintentional. For this, I apologise.

I hope the patience of reading it is tempered by a little pleasure. And that it might embolden you to put your own thoughts on paper!

THE FAMILIES

The Gintys (Office Peon/Hindu Family)
Daughter married. Lives in Hyderabad, India.
Son PRABU (Psychiatrist) married to MOHINI.
Lives in Vancouver, Canada.
Their son, married, lives in the USA.

The Srivastavas (The Judge/Hindu Family)
Son VIR (Businessman) married to MEENA. Lives in Michigan, USA.
Their daughter, married, lives in the USA.

The Agrawals (The Java Salesman/Hindu Family)
Daughter married. Lives in Hyderabad, India.
Son ROOP (Cardiologist) married to MADHURI.
Lives in Georgia, USA.
Their two sons, one married, one single, live in the USA.

The Patels (The Jewelers/Joint Hindu Family)
Son Chandu aka PATEL (Jeweller) married to NALINI.
Lives in Birmingham, UK.
Their son, married, lives in the UK.

The Gopalans (University Registrar/Hindu Family)
Daughter married. Lives in Hyderabad, India.
Son RAMU (Radiologist) married to PADMINI.
Lives in Toronto, Canada.
Their son and daughter, married, live in the USA.

The Sharmas (Public Servant/Hindu Family)
Older son lives in California, USA.
VAS (Engineer) married to SAVITRI.
Lives in Hyderabad, India.
Their daughter and son, married, live in India.

The Mirzas (University Professor/Muslim Family)
Older Son, lives in Hyderabad, India.
Son RASHID (Food Scientist) married to NAIMA.
Lives in a district close to Hyderabad, India.
Their three children live in the USA.

CHAPTER 1

The Conference Call

A sense of ending
In search of a beginning?

It was spring in Toronto. The month was April. The year was 2019.

The snow had nearly melted, and the temperatures were beginning to rise. A cooler air whiffed through the air in High Park, barely a ten-minute walk from Ramu's modest two storey brick house on a quiet road in west village. The tulips were in bloom and the cherry blossoms were in their "pink perfection." They would fall off like snowflakes soon.

Ramu had just gotten off the conference call with his school friends from 1964. The sound of robins and woodpeckers in the background announced the turning over of seasons. A good omen, he thought. They had reconnected after fifty-five years. Seemed like an eon.

Prabu had initiated the call. Because he was based in Vancouver, he had traced them by Google searches, Facebook, and family contacts in India. With changes in names, surnames, and adopted aliases, it was not easy. Vir would be tracked down in Michigan, Patel in Birmingham UK, Roop in Georgia, USA, and Vas in Hyderabad, India. And to his surprise Ramu in Toronto. He felt like a detective trying to locate the suspects while investigating a crime scene.

These were the six partners in crime who had played, studied, explored, eaten, gone to movies, and gawked at girls together. They were inseparable.

The conference call was arranged for noon in North America. It would be five o'clock in the evening for Patel in England. Nine-thirty that night for Vas in Hyderabad. Prabu would initiate the call from Vancouver at nine o'clock in the morning. The six of them would be speaking to each other after five decades. His wife Mohini was excited for him. This would cheer him up, she thought. He had had bypass surgery a couple of months back. It had come unexpectedly—the heart attack, that is.

Five o'clock in the morning on October third, 2018, would be etched in the calendar. It would take its place among family birthdays and anniversaries.

He wasn't sure if he should share the news of his heart attack with his friends on the call. "Not a good icebreaker after fifty-five years," he surmised. Moreover, he was feeling fine, thanks to the cardiac rehab.

The idea of a reunion came to him in a moment of weakness. When he was overcome by a fear of dying. So much to catch up and so little time left. He then began to track them down. He finally located all six of them.

He was thrilled. He hesitated before calling the first number. It was as if he was about to drop a coin in a slot machine without knowing what to expect. Then he punched the numbers on his hand phone, one by one.

"Hi, this is Prabu, is that Ramu?"

"Yes, it's me." There was a slight pause.

"*Arrey Yar*, radio silence from you since 1964!" He shifted the phone against his ear. These new flat phones were so uncomfortable. He missed the curved earpiece of the phones of his childhood.

"Sorry I lost touch."

"Have you been in Toronto all along?"

"Yes. I tried to contact you but didn't have your number."

"Yes, it's a shame. We have been in the same country. Is this convenient?" His wife appeared in the doorway, but he waved her away.

"Yes, we are three hours ahead."

"I know. Must be cold."

"Well, it's cloudy today, but the snow has melted away. Who else is joining

us?"

"The whole gang. Wait, there is someone joining."

"Hello, guys, this is Vas from Hyderabad."

"Oh my! Vas!" Prabu said. "It seems like ages! Lovely to hear your voice."

"Likewise," said Vas.

"What are you doing now?"

"I retired from the Public Works Department as an Electrical Engineer."

"Any kids?"

"Yes, two. Savitri and I are blessed. Arun is a doctor. Lives close by. Daughter Savita is in Bangalore."

"Any grandkids?"

"Yes, Arun has a girl. Savita my daughter is married to a software engineer in Bangalore and has one son."

"Any news of Rashid and Kazmi?"

"Haven't heard from them in ages. Last I heard, they had returned from Haj."

"What did Rashid do?"

"Food Scientist. Worked in the districts. Now retired."

"Where does he live now?"

"Heard he is in Hyderabad, in a retirement home. Unfortunately, we have lost touch."

"How about his kids?"

"Three. All in the USA, I heard."

"How about our other classmates?"

"Some in Hyderabad. Some went to the Middle East. The rest are in U.K, Canada and the USA."

"So, what's new in Hyderabad?"

"Quite a lot. Everyone has become religious. Nobody leaves home without performing *pooja* in the morning. New temples have sprung up everywhere!"

"Hmm, that's interesting," said Ramu. "Is that street side small *Ganesh idol* that we prayed at still there?"

"Yes. They built a huge temple around it."

"Hang on, I hear someone."

"Hello guys, this is Patel from Birmingham." The voice was warm and recognizable. He was the class clown who cracked everyone up with his impromptu jokes.

"Hey this is Ramu. Your accent has changed. You sound British!"

Patel broke into his infectious laughter. "You are kidding me. My white friends tease that I speak English in *gujarati.*"

Everyone chuckled.

"What is your line of work?" asked Ramu.

"Jewelry business. Same as my family in India."

"How are things?"

"Can't complain. Life is first class."

"Good to know that."

"Hello, Prabu this is Vir." His voice was raspier than back then.

"Hi, Vir. Great to hear your voice."

"Same here. So exciting."

"So, you are in Michigan? Ramu, Patel, and Vas are already on the line." Three separate hellos followed in a chorus.

"Yes, I am in Michigan. Sorry I called in a little late. Was on a call with a real estate agent."

"Oh really," said Patel, curious. "Buying property?"

"Yes, we are looking for a beachfront property in Florida. You know the winters are getting harder. Meena has a thyroid condition and I have arthritis. Can't handle the cold."

"Sorry to hear that," said Patel.

"We are okay otherwise. No major health issues."

"Are you retired?"

"Yes. Owned my own company. Now enjoying life."

The phone line clicked. "Hello, this is Roop." A bolder voice replaced the timid one they knew.

"Where are you now?" asked Vas.

"I am in Georgia," replied Roop.

"That is in the south, right?"

"That's correct."

"Heard it is white Christian country."

"That's right. They are very nice. It was a safe place to raise our children."

"Republicans, mainly?"

"Over the years, yes. But demographics are changing."

"Trump supporters?"

"Yes, I voted for him," replied Roop.

"Me too," piped in Vir. Good on taxes and opposed to socialism."

"What's your occupation, Roop?" Prabu asked.

"Cardiologist. I retired last year."

"Oh I could do with your help," Prabu reacted.

"Sorry. Are you not well?"

"Fine now. I had a bypass last winter."

"Sorry to hear that. Glad you are well now. Nice of you to arrange this call," said Roop.

"My pleasure. It is long overdue. All of us are retired and settled. Time to catch up."

"Any kids, Roop?" continued Prabu

"Yes, Madhuri and I have two kids. Both doctors. Arun is in New York and Anoop lives in San Francisco."

"Married?"

"Yes, Arun is married to Melanie. A white girl. Very nice. Loves Indian food. They have two kids."

"And?"

"Oh Anoop is a bachelor, won't commit. it's his life anyway. Can't tell them what to do. Not like our days."

"Agree. Is your wife Madhuri from Hyderabad?"

"No she is from Bombay. We met in Atlanta during residency. It was love at first sight."

"How romantic. What's her speciality?" asked Patel.

"She is a primary care physician," repled Roop.

There was a pause.

Grabbing the moment in an enquiring tone, Prabu said, "I was wondering if we should have a reunion?"

"That is an excellent idea," Vir responded. "I can host you all. We live in the suburbs. We have six bedrooms with attached baths, a four car garage, pool with jacuzzi, sunroom, and a huge deck at the back. The property backs into the woods."

"Wow! Proud of you," Prabu replied. "Nice of you to offer. We will take you up on it."

"Vas, is July convenient for you?" Vir inquired.

"I think so. We have to find someone to keep an eye on our house."

"Where do you live now?"

"Savitri and I live in our old family house in Hyderabad. Two bedrooms, quite spacious. We move into the living room and sofa bed when the kids visit together. Very cozy. The grands love playing in the backyard."

"Yes, I remember your house," said Roop. "I can still taste the *upma* your mom used to make."

"The good old days," said Vas nostalgically.

"How about meeting over the July fourth weekend?" interjected Vir.

"That sounds good," replied Prabu. "You may have to send sponsorship letters to Patel in U.K. and Vas in India for the American Visa. They are very strict since Trump became president."

"Sure thing," Vir shot back.

Then Prabu noted down their addresses.

"Prabu and Vas, you should visit me in Toronto first," suggested Ramu. "We can drive together to Vir's in Michigan for the reunion."

"I will need a letter for the Canadian visa as well," said Vas.

"No problem, Vas. I will send it," reassured Ramu.

"Okay, I am going to start an email thread," announced Prabu. "I am going to call it The Reunion."

"Thanks, Prabu," everyone chimed. And then they hung up.

Prabu sat in his chair, motionless, trying to take a measure of the call.

"So how did it go?" asked Mohini, walking in with his pills and a glass of water.

"Good, I think," he replied. As he downed them one by one with sips of water, he looked through the window. He could see the tree-lined street and the park close by. It was eerily quiet. The sun was forcing its way through the clouds. The silver-clad mountains in the distant horizon glistened from the rays of the sun.

The conference call conjured up images from the past. Of childhood days, school, teachers, and the gang of six. It seemed oceans away in time and space. Like a black and white picture that had lost its gloss to time. A lifeless picture needing new energy and a frame. Two time zones that needed to be pieced together. The past with the present.

FIFTY-FIVE YEARS EARLIER

CHAPTER 2
Hyderabad, India 1964

Life is safe when predictable
With change cometh the unpredictable

It was spring in Hyderabad. The month was February, and the year was 1964. The weather was beginning to warm. Evenings were generally pleasant, with people wearing sweaters to shield themselves from the cold winds.

The Sharmas had lived in Hyderabad for several generations. They considered themselves true Hyderabadis. They were aware of its history, as it had been passed down from generation to generation. Vas's grandfather's usual refrain was "You don't know who you are until you know who you were."

The history of the city dated back to the third century. The region covered much of the central region of the country and the deccan plateau. Various Hindu kingdoms ruled in the subsequent centuries. It went under the control of the Bahmani rule in the fifteenth century. Finally, the independent state of Hyderabad was founded by Quli Qutb Shah in 1591. He built the city around the famous monument of Charminar, which became a centre of culture and commerce. After a brief rule by the Mughals, it was captured by the first *Nizam* in the early eighteenth century. It was the largest princely state as well as the last one to join the republic of India. This piece of history is seared in the consciousness of the city.

The City of Pearls, as it came to be known, was once ranked as the best city to live and work in India. Once you lived in Hyderabad, you fell in love with the city and always wished to return. All cultural festivals like Diwali, Christmas, and Ramadan are celebrated with equal fanfare. The city is known for its *ganga-jamuni tehzeeb*, meaning the confluence of Hindu and Muslim cultures and traditions. Different languages are spoken, including Hindi, Telugu and Urdu, sometimes a hybrid of all three. And English is thrown into the mix for good measure! Local arts, handicrafts and literature reflect the mix of cultures. Being located in the midriff of India, it is a melting pot of sorts. It seems to have absorbed from all the surrounding cultures.

A Hyderabadi it seems is from everywhere, and from nowhere in particular!

In February, daffodils and snowdrops could be seen in the front yards of houses in Vas's locality, with the sweet smell of jasmines in the evening air. Vas, barely fifteen at the time, was walking home from school. It had been a full day of math, physics, and chemistry, the "MPC stream" he had chosen. His father had advised this course, hoping it would lead to a career in engineering. His confident friend Vir chose this avenue of study as well. His friend Patel, who was from a family of jewelers, would choose commerce, while

Ramu, Roop, and Prabu would take the biology, physics, and chemistry stream. That was the "BPC stream" that would lead to a career in medicine. The dye was cast for the gang of six.

With drooped shoulders from the weight of the heavy backpack of books, Vas walked slowly towards home. He looked like a mule on its daily trek with a bag of laundry on its back. The street was lined with shops, some big and some small, with merchandise of different assortments.

There were stalls for clothes, groceries, pharmaceuticals, electronics, jewelry, bangles, books, shoes, betel nuts, tobacco, and much more.

Vas paused at the electronic store, where a bunch of people had huddled with their ears turned to the live commentary from a radio. It was the second cricket test match between India and Pakistan. He spotted Rashid and Kazmi and motioned a hello.

"Pakistan is hundred for one," said Rashid.

"Who got the wicket?" asked Vas.

"Polly Umrigar," replied Rashid.

"Hope they get Wasim out," said Vas.

"He is well settled," replied Rashid.

"Didn't he play for Hyderabad before?"

"Yes. Now he plays for Pakistan."

"Why did he move?" asked Vas.

"Because Pakistan lured him by assuring a spot in the test team," replied Rashid.

"Couldn't the Indian team have selected him to play for them?" asked Vas.

"He wasn't sure. The selectors had others in mind."

"I see. I had better run," said Vas, as he started walking away.
"See you tomorrow at school."
"See you, bye."

The street was crackling with energy. His mood was grim as he thought of what Rashid said. He wore a serious expression on his face. This characteristic would become his identifying mark. "Mr. Serious," he would come to be called. His walk was determined, although his strides gradually shortened with weariness as he reached the public garden road. This was the oldest public park in the city built by the Nizam over a hundred years ago. It was a landmark cue for him that home was just twenty minutes away.

As he began to cross the road, looking left and right, a woman carrying a basket on her head with a baby tucked in a sling around her upper torso passed him. He craned his neck up to see the huge billboard of Dilip Kumar and Madhubala looking longingly at each other with the film title *Mughale Azam* in bold big letters. This was the blockbuster movie of the year in technicolour. Even people from Pakistan came to see their favourite film star Yusuf Khan, aka Dilip Kumar, portray the legendary role of the Mughal prince, Salim, fall in love with a courtesan. It was the famous love story of the sixteenth century.

At the centre of the huge roundabout was an imposing statue of Sardar Patel, the first home minister of a newly born country. He was the architect of the Indian republic who had to overthrow the Nizam of this princely state as he refused to join the union. The Nizam opted to remain autonomous, stay with the British or join Pakistan. None of these options were acceptable to the administration in Delhi. Violence preceded and followed this event.

It was a seminal episode in the region's history.

Vas meandered his way to the other side of the street, weaving through yellow taxis and auto rickshaws. When he got to the other side, he saw the familiar sight of the fruit vendor with her wooden cart of plantains, oranges, and grapes. She was in an animated exchange with a customer who was negotiating the price down.

They finally settled. The vendor bagged the fruit in a paper bag and the man deposited the coins into her outstretched palm. She dropped it into the rusty cash box to join the rest of the takings. Vas passed her after a brief visual exchange to the street on the winding hill leading to his house. There was graffiti on the sidewalk wall, and the white paint was turning yellow due to ageing. Soot had settled on it due to the black fumes spewing out of the vehicular traffic. "Vote for Congress," with the party symbol of the pair of bullocks was painted in red on the wall. As he began to climb the hill, a green double decker bus behind him made its scheduled stop at the public garden gate to release some passengers and collect new ones.

In the backdrop of the entire landscape was the majestic white legislative assembly building. Towering above the melee, it cast a veneer of dignity to the chaos on the street.

Vas trekked up the hill before he reached the entrance to his street beside the state bank of India. As he approached the small island park in front of his house, a dog was scavenging through the garbage dump for food remnants. An empty wooden park bench was tethered to the ground at the centre of the island. It was surrounded by shrivelled up blades of grass.

The sun seemed unforgiving in its disregard for plants, animals, and humans alike.

The Sharmas lived in a modest house. The concrete cemented exterior gave it an appearance of stability. The bedraggled green gate was held together by the two crumbling brick pillars. "Arvind Sharma," his father's name, was etched on the plastered marble plate of the left pillar. His father built this five years ago with a loan from the Cooperative Society.

When Vas opened the gate, he found his grandfather dozing in an easy chair on the porch. His bald head looked shiny like a snooker ball. He wore a serious expression (like himself) with a furrowed face and heavy-lidded eyes. Vas's grandfather woke up with a start after hearing Vas's footsteps. He readjusted his steel-rimmed round spectacles with the wiry stems extending to his ears. On the floor by his side was the Hindu newspaper. He usually plowed through the paper, skimming the headlines first, and then reading the selected articles in detail. He skipped the business page. He loved reading the editorial, usually discussing the opinions with his son. The crossword puzzle was the best, and he saved it for the last.

Sharma Senior had moved in with his son after his wife died of cancer four years ago. Seeing his grandson, he glanced at his gold-plated *HMT* watch to check the time. It was a retirement gift that had not lost or gained a second in all the years he had owned it. His daily routine was fixed like clockwork. He followed it meticulously. He woke up at five, had coffee and breakfast, took a short walk around the block, and had lunch at noon, followed by a short snooze. He had the afternoon tea at three on the porch, lounging in his easy chair while browsing the newspaper. Dinner was at eight, followed by the nine o'clock news. He would turn in around ten. You could tell the time by his daily routine..

Vas bent over and gave him a hug. The familiar smell of his vest exuded warmth.

Squinting his eyes, he said, "*Beta* you are back. How was school?"

"Good Dada," replied Vas.

"What did you learn today?" asked grandpa.

"The Gupta Period."

"Oh, the golden age of India!"

"Yes, the teacher said we made several inventions and discoveries in science."

"Yes, that is correct," nodded grandpa. He continued, "The age of the Nine Scholars. *The Navaratnas.* Did you eat lunch?"

"Yes, Dada."

"Okay, go in and wash your hands," he said as he stroked the stubble on his face. He had worked out that the "7 O'CLOCK" blade (Made in England) would last a fortnight if he shaved only every other day.

The Sharmas were a Brahmin family. Strict vegetarians. Alcohol and smoking were forbidden..

Vas and his older brother Rishi shared a bedroom with their grandfather, sleeping on the floor while he slept on the steel cot that he brought along with him when he moved to his son's place after his wife died. The solid metal furniture was handed down to him by his father.

Rishi had just completed his engineering degree and earned a scholarship to study at Berkeley in the USA. He would leave in a month after getting his visa.

Vas placed his school satchel on the shelf below the table on which sat the National Ekco Radio. An embroidered lace cloth covered it to protect it from dust.

His mother was clad in a red sari. Her face glowed with a bright *sindoor* in the middle of her forehead. Her dark black hair was combed neatly back into a ponytail. Her expressive eyes, perfectly aligned teeth, the gold necklace and bangles gave an aura of traditional elegance. She greeted him with a warm smile, running her hand through his hair, "You look tired."

"I am okay, a little hungry."

"Why don't you sit down? I will make you hot chocolate." Vas went into the kitchen and sat on the floor.

"Your dad will be home soon. You can have dinner with him and grandpa," said Mrs. Sharma.

He said, "Yes," as he sipped the drink.

"Did you get your report card?" she asked.

"Yes."

"How were your marks?"

"Ninety percent in all subjects except Math," he replied nervously.

"How much in Math?"

"Eighty-five percent."

"That's not enough for engineering," she remarked.

"My teacher said he will help me after class."

"That's good," she said.

Then they heard the footsteps. Mr. Sharma and his father were heard chatting. The usual exchange of pleasantries and tidbits about the office.

Mr. Sharma worked in the income tax office. He had joined as a clerk and rose to the rank of officer, a middle management position. He applied for the job of senior supervisor, but was passed over in favour of Mr. Gyaneshwar, who belonged to the scheduled class. A good colleague who had come up through the ranks.

Lamenting, he told his office friends, "Doesn't help if you are a Brahmin."

"Affirmative action to right old wrongs," replied one of his colleagues.

"Whatever," replied Sharma.

The other rumour in the office was that he was passed over as he refused to accept bribes and kickbacks. One needed to go along in order to get along.

"You see, the wheels of the Income Tax department don't turn if you are honest," his colleague Mr. Murthy opined.

Mr. Sharma had reconciled himself to this reality. A spirit of resignation took over. He worked now with little zeal. He was a man in auto mode, mechanical and predictable. He had reached a plateau in his career. This was it. His only goal now was to get his kids married and settled. Pay off the loan. And retire with a pension and provident fund like his father.

He walked in with a jaded look, carrying his leather briefcase. His cotton suit was wrinkled and creased in the sleeves with a patch of sweat in the armpits. He was glad to come out of it.

"*Beta,* how are you? Got your report card?" he asked his son.

"Yes *Pitaji*. I will show it to you."

"How did you do in Math?"

"Eighty-five percent."

"Hmm! Is that enough?"

"No, *Pitaji*."

"So, shall I sit down with you to improve your marks?"

"My teacher said he will help."

"Good, good. You must study hard if you want to get into engineering," he advised.

"Yes *Pitaji*. Can I ask you a question?"

"Yes."

"Our friends want to bike up to Golconda Fort next week. Can I go?"

"Who are all going?"

"Prabu, Vir, Roop, Patel, and Ramu."

"That's your gang, isn't it?"

"Yes, it is," replied Vas.

"Have their parents agreed?" asked Mr. Sharma.

"They will ask today."

Mr. Sharma looked at his wife for a sign. She nodded. "Okay, if they all agree, you can go. What about a bike?" he enquired.

"Rishi said I can take his."

"Make sure the tires are pumped up and the chain oiled."

"Yes, *Pitaji.*"

The Reunion

Turning to his wife, Mr. Sharma asked, "Any news about Rishi's Visa?"

"He has an appointment in the Visa office in Madras in a month," she replied.

"Oh, I see. I have asked for an office loan to pay for his airfare. It will be deducted monthly from my salary until it is fully paid."

"Shall I lay the plates?" his wife asked.

"Yes I will be ready in fifteen minutes."

"Call your grandfather."

"Okay, Mama."

Vas, his dad, and grandpa sat at the dinner table in the kitchen.

His mother served the *chapatis* from the hot plate, followed by *subzi*, rice, and *dal*. Finally, she served *curd rice* to cool things off.

After they had finished, she sat at the table alone and ate.

"So are you going to Golconda?" asked Grandpa.

"Yes. I am going with my friends."

"It was the capital of the old Hyderabad state. That's where the Kohinoor diamond was made."

"Is it still there?"

"No it's on display in the Tower of London. The fort is in ruins. You have to be careful."

"Where is your brother?" he asked

"Rishi is eating out today with his friends after a movie," answered his mother

"We will miss him when he leaves," grandpa said, choking with emotion.

"When he is settled in the US, he can sponsor you. Not much opportunity in India for you Vas," he continued.

"Why do you think so *Dada?*"

"Mr. Nehru is a great man but his politics is socialist. No jobs for the young. There is a rumour he is grooming his daughter," he added, turning to Mr. Sharma.

"Yes yes," said Mr. Sharma, as he pored over the headlines of The Hindu.

"He has also given too much away to the Muslims," continued the grandfather. "They can have many wives and children. They will one day outnumber us and take over the country."

"No, *Pitaji* that will never happen. We are eighty-five percent of the population. Majority, that is," asserted Mr. Sharma.

"Hmm," the senior Sharma exclaimed, unconvinced.

He then walked away to his bedroom and turned on the radio for news.

Mr. Sharma walked out through the grilled kitchen door to the washroom outside. Mrs. Sharma cleaned up the kitchen and settled down to browse a housekeeping magazine. She fantasized about the dream kitchen items in colour. Her wish list was long.

Mr. Sharma changed into his white *pyjamas* and *kurta* for the night. A sense of peace descended on him.

CHAPTER 3

The Monsoon Season

Labours of love can be burdensome
After a long day's toil for some

The sweltering sun in Hyderabad exhausted folks in the towns and villages. Large swaths of land were baking, and parents kept the children indoors to protect them from the blazing sun. Temperatures were surpassing records in the coastal areas typically cooled by the easterly winds. One local news channel called it a "heat bomb" from Pakistan! Vegetable vendors doused their produce with water every fifteen minutes. Fruit vendors wiped their faces and arms with wet towels while day labourers hid under tents during their breaks.

Farmers in villages offered prayers to the rain god *Indra*, the Lord of the sky to protect their crop. Their prayers were answered. Clouds began to form, and water droplets pierced through the warm breeze, getting bigger and stronger by the minute. The heavens finally cracked open with lightning and thunder. Children in villages and towns danced in the rain while adults rejoiced. The rain hit the scorched earth with a force and vengeance. The sound of the downpour with the heavy pitter patter was deafening.

Ramu and Prabu were caught in the rain on their way home from school. Their school uniform of khaki shorts and white shirt with the slightly off-centre blue and gold striped silk tie began to dampen.

They took refuge under the canopy of a small provision store for shade. As rain fell loudly on the metal roof, they could hear frogs freeing themselves through the soil with a croaking sound.

After a half hour, the clouds ran out of water, the drops weakened, and the rain came to a halt. Ramu and Prabu continued their trek home with a spring in their step. As they headed back, they saw a beautiful rainbow on the skydome. When they looked up again a few moments later, it was gone!

They picked up the conversation on the Golconda trip, before the sound of thunder had interrupted it. They squeezed their satchels into their armpits, wrapping their arms tightly around it, to protect it from the thin drizzle.

Revitalized by the shower, the sky looked bluer, washing away all the pollutants in the air. Prabu informed Ramu that he had worked out the directions to the fort with his father. The Golconda adventure would be the big highlight before the final exams. It would be a memory that would last for years to come. They would then part in different ways, to different futures. Some would become doctors, others engineers, and one a businessman.

Ramu's parents, the Gopalans, lived in Shanti colony. Ramu often wondered why they were called colonies! They were, after all, not under the British rule anymore! His father explained that the word can mean a housing project as well. Their colony was a new development. Mr. Gopalan was the registrar of the university. As an administrator, he was responsible for admissions, academic records and credentials, exams, salaries, and promotions. He earned a good reputation for his organizational skills and efficiency. He secured a university housing loan at one percent interest and completed the construction of his house a couple of years earlier. It was a one storey house with provision for a scaled down second floor version in the future subject to availability of funds. He would rent it out. The extra income would be a cushion.

At the next intersection, Prabu took the right turn and Ramu the left. After a good twenty-minute saunter, Ramu reached the archway entrance to his community. The cloth banner "SHANTI COLONY" was suspended from the capstone.

The unpaved street down the slope was flanked by a row of houses on either side. They were in various stages of construction; some were completed, and others were barely above the ground.

The familiar sight of their one storey with a small gate and a compound wall was comforting. He opened the gate and walked up the steps into the grilled entrance door. He announced that he was home, placing his bag in the spandrel under the stairs. The family had been sleeping on the roof lately to escape the oppressive heat downstairs. A plastic sheet covered the mound of sleeping paraphernalia on the landing upstairs. This consisted of sheets and pillows with blankets to cover themselves during the early morning chill. Ramu and his sister Ramani loved nightfall. It thrilled them to lay on their makeshift beds and gaze at the stars.

The Gopalans were proud of their station in life. They were secure with a steady, middle-class income of a thousand rupees a month. Mrs. Gopalan managed the household expenses with three hundred rupees a month. The rest of the seven hundred was earmarked for school fees, paying off the housing loan, making savings and superannuation contributions, and other sundries. Mr. Gopalan's credo was "Plain Living and High Thinking," which he drilled into his children. They were strict vegetarian Brahmins who ate and drank in stainless steel plates and glasses. The silverware was reserved for Mr. Gopalan's father, to acknowledge his rank and age. The glassware crockery was set aside for serving visitors from other castes and religions. Ramu even at this young age wondered that this was odd.

Mr. Gopalan's goal in life was to make Ramu a doctor and marry Ramani into a good family. Ramu attended the Catholic school for boys and his sister went to a nearby school for girls. She hoped to earn a BA in college. Her father encouraged her to learn typing and shorthand as well so that she could get a job in the Secretariat. The extra income would help her husband and his family. He believed that his son Ramu would benefit from the strict discipline enforced in the Christian school. Moreover, there was no religious indoctrination. Only a morning prayer at assembly: "Our Father, Who art in Heaven, hallowed be Thy name; Thy kingdom come." It was a small price, he decided, to pay "for a good education." Besides, the family went on

Saturdays to the nearby *Balaji* temple. This would offset the risk of any Christian influence during the school hours.

Mrs. Gopalan insisted on Ramu and Ramani fold hands in prayer in front of the family shrine in the kitchen every morning. This was a ritual to be followed before they left for school. Inside the shrine were framed pictures of various deities, an oil lamp that she lit every morning after her bath, and sticks of incense and camphor that she burned. She placed the fruit, usually an apple and a few bananas on the silver plate as offering to God. The plate was passed on to her by her mother. It was a precious relic that reminded her of her mother.

Mr. Gopalan's father was a railway man who retired as a controller of the signal division of the South Central railway. He made sure his sons went to university to get Master's degrees. He had pleaded with his British boss, Mr. Edwards to station him permanently in Hyderabad so that their education would not be affected by frequent transfers. Mr. Gopalan's brother also did well by passing the civil service exam. He worked for the foreign minister's administrative staff in Delhi. He was quite proud of both his sons and never missed an opportunity to sing their praises to his friends and colleagues. He stayed with his son in Hyderabad until his death. He had lost his wife to childbirth many moons ago.

The Gopalans were a part of the South Indian Tamil community in Hyderabad and knew all the families. They were *Carnatic music* connoisseurs and attended the annual *Krishna Gana Sabha* winter music festival in the school auditorium. It was a popular annual event that attracted the entire community. Prominent musicians of the day were invited. Budding young artists were encouraged to seek inspiration from them.

Young Ramu, now about sixteen, was busy preparing for the high school graduation exams. He was hoping to earn the marks needed for medical school. The competition was brutal. He would have to score in the nineties in biology, physics, and chemistry to qualify. He studied with Prabu and Vas on the weekends. "Combined studies," as it was referred to, meant one would read while the other took notes, and the third went through the bank of questions from previous years. They would then consolidate their individual contributions into a joint effort. The whole was greater than the sum of the parts.

Ramu chose biology, as he was weak in math. This had a history. As a seven-year-old, when Ramu scored poorly in the math exam, his father approached Mr. Jeevan, his next door neighbour, if he would tutor his son. He taught in the same school.

Mr. Jeevan responded enthusiastically, saying, "Don't worry Mr. Gopalan, send him to me. I will coach him for free." Mr. Gopalan accepted the offer without reservation. He regarded him highly as "an upstanding citizen and a respected instructor in the Boy Scouts Movement." He had complete faith in him.

Ramu went over to Mr. Jeevan's house on the specified evening. His daughter, he learned later, was adopted. Mr Jeevan embraced him warmly and directed him to his office in the corner room while his wife was busy in the kitchen. He was a gaunt looking man with greying, thin hair barely covering his shiny scalp. His glasses were balanced delicately on the bridge of his nose. His piercing eyes and sunken cheeks gave him the appearance of a cadaver.

His wife never came in when he was alone with the kids he tutored. The door was closed during the lessons for complete privacy. He tutored in a darkish room with the window curtain drawn, barely allowing light in. He sat in a reclining chair in shorts and vest with protruding spindly legs. His pupils were made to sit on a stool in front of him. Mr. Jeevan instructed Ramu softly but firmly to follow his instructions. He went through the math problems and equations, stroking him gently on his neck as an encouraging gesture. He released him at the end of the lesson with a hug.

This pattern was repeated over the first week. A routine was established. Ramu told his dad that the lessons were helping him. His father was pleased. The next week Mr. Jeevan drew him a little closer and stroked his thighs. Ramu smartened. He withdrew gingerly, not wanting to upset him. This continued for a few more days until he learned to submit himself to the "groping and stroking" as if it was part of the lesson.

"You must obey the elders," his father had always said.

A couple of weeks later, Mr. Jeevan smothered him more intimately and placed his swelling into his tiny hands. Ramu froze. He was paralyzed with fear. He felt overpowered and trapped. He wanted to run but could not move. Mr. Jeevan left him alone and got up to go into the bathroom outside the door. He returned a few minutes later looking spent. This pattern followed time after time.

Mr. Jeevan told Ramu that he was special, and this was a secret between them. He was not to share this with anyone, not even his parents. Ramu was too afraid to breach the rule.

"I like you," he added. "I will tell your dad you are my favourite student because you are progressing so well. This will make your parents happy."

This was a secret Ramu kept to himself. Only when he was in his forties did he put two and two together. It then dawned on him as to why he was so averse to math.

The awful memory grew over the years like a disease. He was ashamed of it. It was a disgusting episode he could not talk about. It turned into a recurring nightmare that would not leave him, of a dark room with a stiff bony substance on him, that he could not shake off. With this secret, he was alone.

His mind that day was preoccupied with the trip to Golconda. His mother had told him that she would pack *curd rice* with pickles, biscuits, and a banana in the lunch box. As he prepared to sleep, his sister in a half sari helped her mom to tidy up in the kitchen and close shop for the day. She washed the dishes with Palmolive liquid and stacked them in the drying rack placing

the utensils systematically in the allotted sections. The plates were placed side by side vertically, the serving spoons in the upright container, and the larger dishes inverted to drain the water through the gaps in the baseboard.

Mrs. Gopalan stored the pickles, condiments and yogurt in the meat shelf, a meshed wooden cupboard with two levels secured by a door and a latch. She often wondered why it was known as a "meat shelf." After all, they were vegetarians!

The Reunion

As she secured the kitchen door at the end of the day, she felt a sense of satisfaction. It was like drawing the curtains for the day. Like closing a book cover after reading a chapter.

She reminded Mr. Gopalan to pick up some vegetables on his way home the next day. He nodded half heartedly with his attention on the newspaper page before him. He turned the radio on for the Nine PM news. A crackle of thunder and flash of lightning came through the window as he heard the familiar brassy voice on the radio,

"This is All India Radio. Here is the news, by Melville de Mello." He started the broadcast by saying, "There was an exchange of fire across the Indo-Pakistan Border. Two Indian *Jawans* were killed." Mr. Gopalan worried if the war with Pakistan was imminent.

Then came another short burst of rain. Mrs. Gopalan rushed out of the kitchen door and snatched the clothes from the rope line tethered to the mango tree branch and the doorknob. She hung them to dry through the night on the back of the dining room chairs.

Ramu attended to his homework and fell asleep.

Prabu made his way home via the right fork towards Banjara Hills, a relatively new residential area. He lived in the older part of this complex. He waded through the flooded roads with water drains overflowing into tiny little rivulets in search of places to settle. There were broken branches on the street dislodged from the trees by the fierce hurricane like winds.

Electrical lines were damaged with loss of current in many parts of the city. The drainage system constructed some thirty years earlier had not been revamped. A scooter drove through the waterlogged street while a man crossed the road holding his bicycle. The traffic lights were no longer operational. As he walked cautiously trying to avoid a mudslide, a huge lorry drove by splashing a shower of rainwater on him.

He was finally home as he approached the door of his small two bedroom flat in a rundown tenement. The crumbling building had multiple flats, one facing the other, and on either side. Everyone knew everyone. They were dilapidated, low-rent dwellings that his family had occupied for nearly ten years. It was a world within a world. Like living in a bubble. They were tightly packed decrepit units with no infrastructure mostly occupied by the poor.

The 500 units were serviced with common latrines and bathing areas and a running drain carrying black residues. The majority of the tenants were construction workers employed on cheap labour in the new affluent housing development a mile away. Most of the families belonged to the *scheduled class*, the depressed classes as they were known. They were relegated to do the jobs of sweeping, cleaning toilets, weaving baskets and other menial jobs that the upper classes considered beneath their station. They were also called *Dalits*. Gandhi called them *Harijans* or Children of God.

There were some gypsy families as well who wandered from one construction site to another, ending up usually in the fringes of the communities they landed. They were a nomadic community believed to have migrated from Rajasthan, a northern state of India. They were included in the list of *backward classes* by the government. There was an ongoing rift between them and the other scheduled tribes over the criteria for inclusion.

Mr. Ginty advised his son Prabu to apply for his medical school admission in the *scheduled class quota.* "You still have to get at least seventy percent marks," he said. "There is competition even in this group."

"Why is it less for me?" asked Prabu.

"It's a long story. Go read about Ambedkar, whose picture is on the wall," Mr.Ginty replied.

"Who was he?" asked Prabu.

"A social reformer. Like a father to our people. He wrote our rights into the constitution. He was a founding father of independence."

Prabu began to realize early on that life was not going to be easy for him. He noticed that his father and mother worked much harder than his friends' parents. He needed to work hard as well in order to succeed.

Mr. Ginty worked as a *peon* in the principal's office at the nearby government school. His mother worked as a cleaning woman. His job was of a "glorified office boy" with a uniform and a title. He had to clean the office furniture, sort documents, arrange them neatly in the tray, make tea, courier papers between offices, and triage visitors seeking access to the principal. He was on a small salary with pension benefits.

His mother worked in three brahmin households. She was not allowed in their kitchens. Her job was to wash clothes, sweep and mop the floors, and run errands for them. She walked the two kilometres back and forth. She had to be punctual like clockwork or would get yelled at for coming late.

His sister Swarna helped her mom in the cleaning of houses. She would sweep the floor while her mother washed the clothes or cleaned the dishes. It saved time. She was expected to be on time for the next house.

Prabu had mentioned the trip to the Golconda Fort the day before to his father. He said he could use his bike and he would walk to the office that day. The family huddled in the tiny kitchen to share the dinner of *chapati,* rice, *dal,* a leftover takeaway from one of the houses she had cleaned, and yogurt. This was a daily staple with little variation except for a piece of mutton or chicken thrown in now and then.

They ate in silence. Then Prabu sat down to do his homework. They were all tired. The day ended like the day before and the day before that. Sleep awaited them with open arms. Tomorrow would be an identical day.

CHAPTER 4
Business As Usual

Do we make our circumstances?
Or are we made by them?

Hyderabad is a melting pot, Mr. Husain, the history teacher, had often taught the boys. Hindus and Muslims, Christians and Parsis, Punjabis and Gujaratis all lived together and got along. People spoke different languages like Hindi, Urdu, Tamil, Telugu, Gujarati, or Punjabi, depending on their mother tongues. The educated spoke English as well. It was referred to as Hinglish, a portmanteau of Hindi and English. Even the uneducated dabbled in a smattering of it. Translanguaging was common with people. They took a sentence from one language and mixed it with another from a different language. Patel's *gujarati* community was part of this diversity.

The Patel brothers lived in the heart of the old city. They were a joint family. Their bungalow was in the midst of a slew of shops. In a bylane of electronic shops, clothing merchants, jewellers, pharmacies, general stores, and a vegetable market. They were engulfed by the smell of fruit, vegetables, human sweat, and body odor. The *Gujarati School* in the neighborhood had educated generations of residents for over fifty years. The Patel family had migrated from Gujarat, a western state, some hundred years ago and established themselves as jewelers. The settlement was called a *Samaj,* meaning community.

The narrow streets and lanes were awash with puddles after the heavy rains. The clouds looked dry with the last drop of rain squeezed out of them. The leaves on the trees looked greener, having been cleansed of the dust and pollution. Rickshaw drivers were struggling to pull their passengers through the wet streets, their leg veins bulging due to the weight. Smiling kids in green and white uniforms walked hand in hand as they walked through the cracks and puddles on the street.

The Patel family lived in a two-storey bungalow, an ancestral home that their great-grandfather had bought many moons ago. The house grew as bedrooms and toilets were added to accommodate the growing family. A coat of fresh paint every few years gave it a "face lift" to conceal the blight of ageing. This happened at Diwali, the Festival of Lights, when it was time to close the year-end accounts and open a new one. To bring a closure to what has been and make a new beginning.

Kantibhai, the oldest of the brothers and the patriarch of the family, occupied the largest bedroom with his wife and their two children. Rank and status came with age. Baldevbhai and his wife took the second large bedroom with their son (Chandu, aka Patel). The youngest brother occupied the smallest bedroom with his wife and children.

The two bathrooms were shared between the three families. They were a traditional family in which hierarchy determined each member's role and responsibilities. Everyone stayed within their assigned positions and kept within their lanes.

Fifteen-year-old Chandu, known as Patel to his friends, often felt excluded and ignored due to his placement in the family. He often felt unmoored. In some ways, this worked to his advantage, as he felt "loose and free," with nothing specific expected of him. This came out in his personality as someone who didn't take himself too seriously and was able to joke and laugh when things got tense. His funny one-liners were part of the class folklore.

The brothers deferred to Kantibhai for all major decisions involving money and family matters. Disagreements were never voiced. The women in the family consulted his wife Meenaben, the matriarch, for guidance. It was a common kitchen where she decided the groceries needed for the menus of the day. She decided the servant assignments. She also oversaw the arrangements needed for celebrating family birthdays and important festivals.

The cousins followed the family ethos, with Dilip enjoying superior status as the son of the patriarch and the eldest among the siblings. With all the "nuts and bolts" aligned, the unit functioned like a well-oiled joint family machine.

The jewelry store in the old city had brought prosperity and security to this generation, the generation before, and the generation before that. Kantibhai, who was austere in his outlook, dressed spartanly in a white *kurta* and *dhoti* and wore a *Gandhi* cap. During the winter months, he wore a woolen vest.

Decisions about inventory, pricing, and ensuring they were properly stocked were left to him. He had refined this over the years, perfectly balancing income with expenses, and allowing for a net profit of twenty percent. The demand for gold and silver, rubies and emeralds, and pearls had lately spiked in a big way. By studying the ledger book, he had worked out that the months of January, February and March were the most lucrative. To outdo the competition, he launched a new scheme, called "Try before you Buy," to attract new customers. This tactic moved the old inventory off the shelves so that he could refresh it with newer designs.

"A risk worth taking," explained Kantibhai. It would catch the attention of clientele they had built over the years by earning their trust and confidence: families they knew and who knew them.

"Gujarati Brothers. Established in 1901. Appointed by HRH, The Nizam of Hyderabad," appeared on the storefront banner, illuminated with flickering blue and green light bulbs at night. The catchy brand name was also embossed on the plastic cases and the blue velvet inside of the jewelry boxes used to pack the sold items. It added a touch of distinction.

The brothers tried hard to remain competitive by creating new designs, offering discounts and payment schemes, and remaining solvent with at least a twenty percent profit on every merchandise item they sold. Patel Brothers Jewellers was now a household name. They took pride in displaying the items in the store in the glass cabinets. The expensive pieces were in the drawers under lock and key. They were visible through the transparent glass tops and were delicately extracted with forceps for inspection whenever a customer requested it.

There was a small workshop at the back of the store with Jaggubhai, now in his fifties, stringing pearls, cutting diamonds, making necklaces, chokers, and earrings, and repairing fancy watches. He was the superb goldsmith who created magic with his deft hands and keen eyes for detail. He melted and recast gold into new shapes and designs. This alcove was the epicentre of the store. Jaggubhai was treated like a member of the family and was included to partake of the lunch packed for the brothers. He was a middle-aged man who looked older than his age with a subservient disposition and apologetic stoop. His weary face with pale eyes and sunken cheeks denoted premature ageing due to the strain of an occupation that demanded precision.

He knew his place in the family. He was essential but unequal in pecking order. He knew the boundaries and never crossed them.

A uniformed security guard stood at the entrance of the store with a short staff, monitoring the comings and goings, accepting tips from them, and making them feel valued and important. He greeted them with a bow and salute.

They had four salespersons in the store, all dressed in black *jodhpuris,* corralling customers to their section of the jewelry. A little boy in shorts offered hot tea in winter and cool *Fantas* in summer to everyone who walked by, as a hook to draw them in.

The Patel brothers walked in step with Kantibhai ahead and the others behind him. They removed their *chappals* at the door. The doorman collected them in a bag and stored it away on the side. They walked straight to the recessed arched nook adjacent to the workshop. It displayed the portrait of the grandfather who had founded the store many decades ago. A garland of roses adorned the frame. In the sacred sanctum were idols of various deities placed on tiny brass plates. Sticks of incense jutted out of a lotus shaped wooden holder. Rose petals were strewn for fragrance. Kantibhai lit the silver lamp every morning before opening the business to the public. The three brothers put their hands together and closed their eyes in prayer. This ritual was performed daily like the brushing of teeth before having a cup of tea in the morning.

Chandu who came to be known by his family name Patel and the cousins were driven to school daily by Ramlal the driver. They had switched to the catholic institution after having completed middle school in the neighborhood *gujarati school* for better instruction in English. Kantibhai maintained that a working knowledge of English was essential for the business.

Ramlal the driver was a man in his sixties who had been in the employ of the family for nearly twenty-five years. He drove the Studebaker car that had served the family faithfully. The car was an American import that the older Patel had purchased second-hand. He washed the car daily and polished it with a chamois leather cloth made of sheepskin. The condition of the car defied its age. It was betel green in colour with grey trims. It was Ramlal's pride and joy. He looked after it like a baby.

Patel got dropped at the boy's school first with his cousins. Before getting off the car, Patel said, "Ramlal, you know I am going to Golconda on my bike?"

"Yes *Baba*, your mother informed me. You have to be careful. The roads are in shambles after the rain. You should look out for the ditches. I will see to your bike and make sure there is no puncture."

"Thank you, Ramlal."

Ramlal then drove away, carrying his precious cousin Nalini to the girls' school for the next drop off a mile away.

Patel ambled straight to the gang huddled in a corner. Rashid was with Kazmi just a few paces away. Close by, but not so close. Like the second tier. He gestured a greeting to them and paused briefly. Then he joined the gang.

Vas, Ramu, Prabu, Roop, and Vir were going over the route for their trip, with Prabu animatedly drawing directions in the air and pointing his fingers in various directions. He punctuated the hand signals with landmark names like the police station, the Taj Hotel, the huge billboard, etc., where they needed to go straight or take a right or left turn. The others imagined the route by following Prabu's hand signals seriously, as if their life depended on it.

Roop cut into the conversation, adding, "My dad said to avoid the Lakdi Ka Pul bridge, as it will be fraught with hazards."

They agreed.

The rains usually took the toll on the bridge by widening the cracks and eroding the asphalt patches. The ditches jolted the bikes and rickshaws off course. Accidents were common during the rainy season. The constant and

41

unrelenting traffic claimed more than a few casualties by the end of the rainy season.

"We will go under the bridge through the side streets," said Prabu. By now he was the unofficially endorsed leader of the pack.

"We can stop halfway at the Banjara Hills police station for lunch," he added.

"That's a good idea," Ramu piped up.

"Let's meet at 6 a.m. on Sunday at the bridge?" Prabu informed.

"Yes," they echoed.

They headed to the classroom for the history lesson with Mr. Hussain. Each of them was from a different background, yet a thread of culture seemed to tie them. They were different in their personalities. Vas was rooted, Prabu a leader, Ramu cautious and careful, Roop hardworking and practical, Patel business-like and funny. Vir was the most confident of all, not hesitating to take a risk if needed. They were all cut from a similar cloth, but of different shades of colour.

Prabu and Rashid had developed an exclusive friendship of their own. This was special and separate from that of the gang of six.

They had both walked over to Rashid's place in the old city the other day as he invited Prabu for the first day of *Ramadan*. The road leading to his house was narrow with deep potholes, the street wide enough for only one vehicle like a rickshaw or scooter to pass through at a time. One had to weave his way this way and that before passing through. The house seemed wedged in the space between two similar looking houses. The size seemed more important than the shape. It was clean and tidy. A line of shoes invited him to the door. A worn carpet with faded Islamic motifs welcomed them in. There were prayer mats everywhere. A picture frame with Arabic letters was displayed prominently in the living room.

"*Allahou Akbar*" resounded through the air, beckoning the Muslim community to prayer, a clarion call from the nearby mosque in the Charminar area. It was a monument built in 1591 with four symmetrical arches and pillars made of granite and limestone on the bank of the Musi river. The pillars narrowed into minarets and steeples as they pierced the skyline. This was the centre of the city in the sixteenth century. A clock face on each of the four sides of the monument kept time. A Hindu temple at the foot of the monument had become a source of conflict between the two communities. There was controversy regarding its history and origins. The mystery temple and the famed mosque became part of the local folklore. The advantage of a long passage of time it seems, is that smaller fault lines of history get smoothened over. The community lived in harmony despite some cultural differences.

The Charminar had become an iconic symbol of sorts of the city's complex heritage. Surrounded by a bazaar which buzzed with shops and people, the energy was palpable. Stores sold bangles, pearls, gifts, kebab and chai, dainty crockery, fresh flowers, vintage coins and much more. It was built by the Qutb Shahi king when he shifted the capital from Golconda to the city. It was called the Arc de Triomphe of the east.

Everyone who heard the muezzin call dropped whatever they were doing to kneel down in prayer. Rashid's mother, who was wearing a headscarf, excused herself for a few minutes. When she returned, she greeted Prabu with a smile and a hug and invited him to wash his hands and feet in the bathroom. There was a small bucket with water below the tap which he inverted on his feet and then soaped up his hands with the small piece of Hamam soap left in the chipped plastic dish. He wiped his hands dry with the small cotton hand towel that hung from a nail on the wall.

When he emerged from the bathroom door, Rashid's mother motioned him to sit down on the mat. She offered him dates and biryani rice with chickpeas, fried eggplant curry, and mutton. All were neatly arranged on a family porcelain plate. A similar plate was arranged for Rashid as he came out of the bedroom after his prayer.

Rashid's older brother Karim was at college. He was five years older than Rashid and was studying for a Bachelor of Science degree. He had been disinterested and sad lately. His relationship with a Hindu girl had broken up. They had been seeing each other for several months. They had fallen in love at the college. They met secretly at dusk in a secluded park, avoiding public places, and arranging their rendezvous carefully with precision.

This worked until they were spotted by her brother, and all hell broke loose. A perfect storm erupted. She was warned by her parents to terminate it, pronto. There was bitter opposition from both sides. Huge arguments broke out about religion and conversion. Both sets of parents were incensed. This was a line that was not to be crossed. You did so at your own peril. The Mirzas arranged for the imam to drive some sense into him. The girl's parents took her to the temple to pray for wisdom. They had reached a point of family intransigence.

Finally, the lovers met one last time and decided that they could not continue and stopped seeing each other. It was too heavy a price to pay. Both sides of the family were relieved.

Prabu felt welcome by Rashid's mother. She had offered the food in their family porcelain. He remembered the meal he had had with Ramu's family just a week ago, sitting outside the kitchen, and eating the meal of rice and vegetable in the glassware crockery while Ramu ate from a stainless steel plate. The difference in treatment confused him. He was the same person in both places, and he received a half welcome in one and a full one in another. He wasn't sure why or what to make of it, or if it should upset him. It was something that would, however, remain with him for years. It would remind him of who he was and where he came from. This would preserve his connection with both Ramu and Rashid, but in different ways.

He offered Rashid an invitation to join them on the bike trip. But Rashid said he was busy with *Ramadan* and wouldn't want to ride while fasting. Prabu felt guilty that they did not plan properly. Perhaps they could have gone after the fasting month?

After school that day, the gang had gone to bed wondering about the trip and what excitement it would bring. It was a memory in the making.

CHAPTER 5

The History Lesson

Every action has a reaction.
Lack of reaction tantamounts to inaction.

The boys walked into the classroom as the bell rang to signal the beginning of a new period.

Mr. Husain was already seated at his desk with the blackboard behind and his notes in front of him.

Rashid and Prabu made their way to the front of the class. Ramu, Roop, Patel, and Vir sat in the row behind and Vas in the row on the right beside them. This was a practised routine. Mr. Hussain picked up the duster and wiped the board clean of the remnants of the previous science class by Mr. Tuljaram, clearing equations, tables, and diagrams. He then wrote the topic "Hindu-Muslim Unity," the words squeaking as the chalk grazed the blackboard.

He cut through the continuing chatter, announcing, "Boys I am going to mark your attendance."

A hush broke through the room.

He started calling names alphabetically, lifting his head each time to confirm if the response matched the name he called. He paused after checking the last name on the list. Seizing the silence, he stood up and said, "I am going to talk to you today about two important periods in our history. The first War of Independence in 1857, and the Razakar Movement in our state following independence in 1947. This will give us a history of Hindu-Muslim relations."

Mr. Hussain was a man in his thirties, of average height and slender build, with an angular face and deep-set eyes. He sported a pencil thin moustache that was precisely trimmed. He donned a blue jacket and black pants with a white shirt and a green tie held together by a steel clasp. He looked compact and collected. Running his finger over his moustache, he said, "We will first discuss the War of Independence in 1857." He then began to read the following notes he had prepared for the class. He had also Xeroxed six copies. One was to be shared between six students. Vas took the copy from Mr. Husain on behalf of the gang of six. It read as follows:

Indian War of Independence 1857

"Hindu- Muslim unity" as a concept was promoted by various leaders like Gandhi and Khan Abdul Ghaffar Khan. The Hindu and Muslim political parties in India were unified in their opposition to the British.

In the first war of independence in 1857, Hindus and Muslims fought alongside each other against the British East India company. The war began in Meerut and spread to other cities like Delhi. Hindu and Muslim peasants and landlords were opposed to the heavy taxes imposed by the East India company. Large numbers of *sepoys* from the Hindu, Muslim and Sikh communities were deployed from the peasantry.

The British realized that the only way to continue their rule was by dividing us along religious and communal lines. "Divide and rule" was their motto. A political strategy to retain power by nurturing disunity among opponents. Muslim leaders however saw through this and proclaimed that the religious and political duty of the Muslims was to fight alongside the Hindus and Sikhs. They emphasized that this was their duty as ordained by the Almighty.

The British became concerned and felt threatened by this. They decided to stir up trouble between the two communities. They introduced cartridges lubricated with the fat of cows and the fat of pigs. This touched a religious nerve. The former was derogatory to the Hindus, and the latter vexing to the Muslims. Both Hindu and Muslim soldiers refused to bite off the sealed beef or pork ends of the cartridge to empty the gunpowder into the barrel. This caused unrest in several places. The British also drilled Muslims into thinking that they would lose their identity in a free India if it were dominated by Hindus. Seeds of a "two-nation theory" were thus sown.

The Muslim soldiers did not fall for this. In fact, they united forces against this ploy. They fought alongside Hindus for the common cause of freedom.

Up until 1857, there were hardly any communal problems. The two communities respected each other. They celebrated both traditions. Hindus took part in *Eid* and Muslims in *Holi* and *Diwali* ceremonies.

This mutiny brought to an end the British East India company and the rule of the Mughals. The British crown took over from the East India company. The great uprising of 1857 is an important landmark in our history that reminds us that we can be stronger when we stand united.

Mr. Hussain put his notes down, wiped a tear from his eye, and said, "I have two questions for you. What were the reasons for our unity before 1857? What are the lessons we can learn from it today?" He picked up his notes to continue. "I am going to talk to you now about Indian Independence in 1947 and the Razakar Movement in 1948."

Indian Independence in 1947 and The Razakar Movement in 1948

On the fifteenth of August 1947, India won independence from the British. They had ruled for almost 200 years. There was a lot of tension between Hindus and Muslims in the months leading up to it. There was growing suspicion. Communities that had co-existed for hundreds of years started attacking one another. Gandhi tried to keep the country together but failed to convince the two sides to compromise. The decision was made to partition India.

Sir Cyril Radcliffe, a British civil servant, was appointed to draw an arbitrary line on the map to divide the country. It was done expeditiously. The line he drew cut towns and villages into two. It also severed families and friends.

The Reunion

The partition plan was completed in five weeks with the approval of Lord Mountbatten, the last Governor General of India. The country was split into two nations. India had a Hindu majority, and Pakistan had a Muslim majority. Then the great migration began from opposite sides of the divide. Sectarian violence broke out in the crossing and thousands were killed. A dark chapter in history.

Jawaharlal Nehru became the first Prime Minister of India and Mohammed Ali Jinnah the first Governor General of Pakistan. About 500,000 people died in the communal riots that followed.

"A year later, another massacre occurred in Central India," continued Mr. Hussain. "It was in our Hyderabad."

Hyderabad was one of the 500 princely states. All the other states had joined the republic in 1948, a year after independence. But the Nizam of Hyderabad, the last of the princely ruling dynasty refused to join the union. This created a chasm in a state where Hindus and Muslims had lived together for hundreds of years. The Nizam entertained the options of remaining with the British, remaining independent, or joining the newly created nation of Pakistan. This outraged the new Indian leaders in Delhi.

Facing an uprising by the Hindu majority, the Nizam ordered the paramilitary wing of his militia, called the Razakars, to muzzle them. This led to brutal violence against the Hindus. The Razakars went from village to village, murdering, pillaging, and plundering temples. There were also incidents in the city. This continued until the Indian army intervened in what came to be known as "Police Action." They routed the Razakar forces and liberated Hyderabad from the control of the last Nizam. In the police action, there was arson, looting, and violence. Thousands of Muslims were killed. Both episodes were traumatic and gruesome.

Mr. Hussain added, "There were hundreds of stories and reports of how Muslims protected their Hindu friends from the Razakars and how Hindu families protected their Muslim friends from the police action." Mr. Hussain put his notes down and wiped his glasses. Speaking in a funereal tone, he added, "Interesting that the British could not divide us in 1857, but split us up so easily in 1947! Now I have two more questions for you. What do you think happened to Hindu-Muslim unity in the years between 1857 and 1947? Are we now one nation or a country of two nations? We will discuss your answers in the next class. You might want to consult your parents, as they may remember these times."

The class fell into silence as the bell rang, bringing the history lesson to a close. A sense of poignancy hung in the air.

Mr. Hussain collected his belongings and left. Rashid and Kazmi left the room together. The gang of six followed.

As Vas returned home, his grandfather dozing on the porch in his easy chair opened his eyes.

"*Beta*, how was school?"

"We learned about the Razakar movement," replied Vas.

"Oh!" he exclaimed with a puzzled expression.

"Do you remember it?" asked Vas.

"Of course I do. I was attacked." And he parted his hair to reveal the scar.

"Hmm I am sorry. How old were you?"

"In my late forties."

"Why do you think it happened?" asked Vas.

"The Razakars were a brutal force. They wanted to silence the Hindus and support the Nizam."

"Did you want to join the Indian Republic?"

"Yes, of course. It was my country that was just born. Why would I want to be part of Pakistan?" He sounded indignant.

Vas took this as a cue to end the conversation and went inside.

Rashid learned upon returning home that his father had also been attacked as he was riding his bike home from college at the age of twenty-five. Mr. Mirza taught economics at the nearby City College and had been promoted to the rank of professor recently. Osman Mirza was a tall and handsome man dressed in a black *sherwani* and a *fez* cap. His nature was as gentle as his face. The high cheekbones lent him an air of maturity.

He was born and raised in the old city and came from a family line of teachers. He married Mehrunissa at her tender age of twenty. Their son Karim was born a year later, with Rashid arriving three years after. They were a close-knit family, law-abiding, and religious. They loved Hyderabad dearly and felt that they belonged.

Mr. Mirza winced a little as he mentioned the assault so many years ago, as if he could still feel the pain. Rashid understood his hesitation to continue the conversation.

Neither his father nor Vas's grandfather had ever mentioned their hurt to anyone before.

A silent memory that was buried deep and better left undisturbed. A hornet's nest better not opened. But it was still pulsating with life.

CHAPTER 6
The Judge and The Java Man

History that we inherit in our years
Are choices made by our forebears

After the class, Roop and Vir ambled along the riverbank toward their homes. Their families knew one other. They both looked preoccupied.

As they pondered over the history lesson, they wondered if it meant anything to them, or if it was a remote piece of history that should not concern them. Their shoulders were slumped with a feeling of fatigue. They had just enough energy left to get home. The traffic was slow but steady with buses and cars crisscrossing and carrying people to their destinations.

Panhandlers weaved their way through the traffic to reach for a coin or rupee from an obliging passenger. Resolute vendors competed with one another to sell their fruit, roasted corn, or peanuts from their baskets. A stray dog and cow coursed leisurely through the street, quite oblivious to the danger of being struck by a vehicle.

Vir said bye to Roop as they reached the Ram Nagar roundabout. Vehicles entered it on the left and drove around until they found their lane to exit. It was a type of circular intersection in which traffic flowed in one direction around a central island. It was a legacy left over from the days of the Raj. The Brits maintained that it maximized safety, minimized delay, and decreased fuel consumption. There was also a saving of electricity, they claimed, as there was no traffic light.

A police officer stood on a stool at the centre of the island. He wore a khaki uniform and a peaked cap, and the insignia on his badge indicated his constable rank. The shiny brown leather belt held his slim waist in place. He waved his baton with authority as he directed the flow.

Vir made his way gingerly to take the second street on the right, while Roop took the third to get to their respective homes. Their images got smaller and smaller until they vanished from each other's sight.

The Jubilee Hills housing development had sold an entire division to the state government to build new villas for judges. Slightly off the beaten path, it was on a secluded street tucked away from the rest of the houses.

Vir's father, Mr. Srivastava, had served in the district courts before he got a chance to work under Justice Das. Mr Das was a man with a reputation for being above reproach. He was both feared and admired. When a vacancy arose in the Hyderabad High Court, he recommended Mr. Srivastava to the Chief Justice. This was approved by the Governor, who was a classmate of his from the college days. One had pursued law and the other had joined politics. Both rose through the ranks to reach their venerable positions.

Mr. Srivastava had now been a judge for three years. After earning a reputation for being thorough, he applied the law meticulously to the evidence, and adjudicated with utmost fairness and diligence. His customary refrain was "I am not here to do justice, I am here to uphold the law." His docket overflowed with cases pending from years of backlog. He tried his best to move the wheels of justice a little swifter than his other colleagues on the bench.

A uniformed guard opened the gates as Vir arrived at the villa. As an only child to his parents Vir was the centre of everyone's undivided attention. He was accustomed to getting whatever he asked. His mother doted on him, but his father insisted that he work hard for the perks lavished in return. He encouraged him to set goals in life and work hard to achieve them. Vas often felt that his father was too perfect a role model to mirror. He decided early on that he was going to chart his own course. He was not going to remain in his father's shadow.

"*Baba*, I hope you enjoyed the day?" enquired the guard.

"Yes, I did. We had an interesting history class. Have you heard of the Razakar Movement?"

"Not me *Baba*. But my father once told me that his sister was violated in the village as she was going to the market."

The guard relieved him of his backpack and opened the front door for him. He placed the bag to the side and walked back to his post.

Hearing the creak of the door, Mrs. Srivastava emerged from the kitchen with a smile. She was a slightly built lady in her thirties dressed in a flowing *Salwar Kameez*. She carried the confidence of someone who has had an easy life without the pressures of living experienced by many others.

"*Beta*, how are you? You look tired."

"I am okay, Ma."

"Did Roop walk with you?"

"Yes, he did."

"Go wash your hands, I will get you a snack and drink."

"Okay, Ma."

Vinod, the cook, a young man in his twenties, overheard the conversation and started preparing a plate for Vir. Servile in his demeanour, he looked weighed down by his role and duties. He was in the process of making the dinner meal for the family. Mrs. Srivastava customarily summoned him to her room after breakfast, lunch, and dinner to dictate the menu for the next meal. He took the orders with his head bowed and his body straddling the entrance, half outside and half inside. No questions were asked except to inform her if he was short of any vegetables or ingredients.

He came to them as a young boy from the village when they were in the district. Mrs. Srivastava trained him to cook as per her family tastes and tradition. He was like a part of the furniture which moved with the family from the district to the city a couple of years ago. The Srivastavas took care of him, attended to all his needs, and fed and clothed him. He kept only a tenth of his salary and sent the remainder to his family in the village. His parents relied on him and his brother who worked as a labourer to fend for them and their two unmarried sisters. They would have to bank some money to get them married into good households in the village.

Srivastas' guests often complimented Vinod on his culinary skills. He acknowledged them reverentially with hands folded and a slight smile. He slept in the servant's quarters in the backyard, a corner he retreated to at the end of the day that was his home and castle.

Mr. Srivastava was punctual about dinner at seven. He expected to eat at the dining table with his wife and son. Dinner was a meal he looked forward to, to get a measure of how things were domestically, to find out if his wife needed anything, and if his son was working hard enough at school. He wore a different hat at home but with equal sway. He moved between his professional and private jurisdictions with fluidity and ease.

Vinod had prepared a standard vegetable meal of hot *chapatis*, two *sabzis*, *dal*, rice, *raita,* and a sweet to finish the meal. Today the dessert was *gulab jamun*, the judge's favourite.

Srivastava came from a *kayasth* family. They were an educated class of Brahmins descended from the *kshatriya* or warrior class of the caste system. Like Vir, he too had been the only son to his parents who were respected by the community. His father was a well-known lawyer with a huge clientele. He impressed upon his son early on that he was expected to inherit his practise and pick up the occupational mantle from him. After his law graduation, they arranged his marriage with Kavita, who was the daughter of a successful business family that made a fortune in the luggage business.

They were the only store in town. Aptly they called it "Lucky Store," a name that everyone in town associated with a suitcase!

Kavita was the third in her family of four. Like her two sisters, she was expected only to get a high school education. She, like her sisters, grew up in a family of love and kindness. Her mother groomed her from her early teenage years to be a good wife and daughter in law. Just as her own mother had trained her many years ago. Kavita was conscious early on that her role would be different from her brother's. He would keep the family name while she would assume that of her husband's. When a suitable alliance was found, she would take the dowry to her new family while her brother at his marriage would receive one from his bride's side.

A suitable boy from the Srivastava family was found. No dowry was expected or given, and the match was arranged. They had been happily married ever since.

The Srivastava family credos, often repeated by the judge's father, and now also by him, included, "Honesty is the best policy. Procrastination is the thief of time. Actions speak louder than words," and many more. Vir knew these proverbs by heart. They spoke to him from time to time as epiphanies.

The judge was strict about his upbringing and drew clear boundary lines. He enforced the rules consistently. There were clearly prescribed consequences for straying. Mr. Srivastava had earned the admiration of everyone in society and Vir would simply be known as "Srivastava's Son." It felt like a crown of thorns. With privileges, yes, but also expectations. There was

The Reunion

little leeway with no elbow or breathing room. Like a ship that had to sail as directed by a compass.

The judge walked in precisely at six-thirty that evening, and the entire household went on high alert. The official driver followed him carrying his bulging briefcase of files. He placed it on his office table and went back to the car. He parked it carefully in the allotted space in the compound.

Mr. Srivastava refreshed himself and emerged from the bedroom in his red silk house coat over his grey pyjama suit. He sat at the dining table upon which three stainless plates and glasses with water had been neatly laid out by Vinod. A cloth napkin accompanied each of the three plate settings. He began to browse the Hindustan Times that was placed on the table. Mrs Srivastava and Vir joined him shortly after.

Vinod started serving the meal items in sequence. *Chapatis, subzi,* rice, *dal,* yogurt, and dessert in that order. He stood in the corner, carefully monitoring their progress, ready to jump in to replenish, or serve the next item on the menu.

Sipping water from the glass, the judge turned to Vir. "Vir, what did you learn today?"

"Papa, Mr. Hussain taught us about Hindu-Muslim Unity."

"That's good, what did you learn from it?"

"That things were good in 1857 but went bad in 1947."

"Yes, yes, we have had some problems, but we should learn to accept each other."

"Papa, Mr. Hussain asked what happened between the two historic incidents."

"Many things. Politics, religion, and unwillingness to compromise."

"Do you have good Muslim friends, Papa?"

"Of course. Shah Wali and Amjad Khan are among my best friends. They were my classmates in school."

"You mean Amjad uncle, who you send sweets to on Eid?"

"Yes. He sends us sweets for Diwali. Do you have any Muslim friends?" the Judge enquired.

"Yes, Rashid and Kazmi. But Roop, Ramu, Prabu, Patel and Vas are closer."

"Why is that?"

"I am not sure. Just happened."

"You should make an effort to get to know them equally well."

"I will try Papa."

"Do you get cases where you have to decide between Hindus and Muslims?" Vir was curious.

"Yes, all the time. I have to decide according to the law."

Vir then remembered about their Golconda trip. He told his dad, "We want to ride to the Golconda Fort."

"That's a good excursion. An educational trip. Do you know the history of the fort?"

"Not much. We heard it is in ruins."

"You should read about it first. First Hindus and then Muslims built it."

"Okay, Papa."

"I will prepare some notes for you and your friends to read."

"Thanks, Papa."

"Tell *Babu* to inflate the tires and oil the chain and levers."

"Will do, Papa."

The conversation began to wane as the judge delved into the newspaper. "Now go do your homework," he directed.

Vir got up from the table and reached out to *Babu,* the male servant to attend to the bike.

Mrs. Srivastava grabbed the moment to ask the judge, "Do you think it is safe for him to bike that far?"

"Yes. Yes, he will be all right. Good for him to learn about our history."

"By the way Roop's parents have invited us for tea tomorrow," she informed him.

"Good, we can discuss the trip with the Agrawals tomorrow. Tell the driver to come tomorrow around two to take us. Give him an extra twenty rupees, as it is a Saturday."

"Yes, I already have."

He then put on the thin-rimmed glasses on his owlish face. His eyebrows began to narrow as he concentrated on the newspaper. His was a cultivated life of routine with few distractions. A secure life of status and authority. He was aware of his station in life and that it was above the common fray. He was cognizant of being in a position of making decisions that would affect lives. It was a burden he had so far carried with honour. He took himself seriously.

Roop made his way lazily to his home. There was a change of pace in his walk since he parted company with Vir at the fork. They were no longer bound by common purpose. He felt free as a free agent.

Mr. Agrawal, his father, had purchased the house five years ago. It was a bungalow that stood in a row of similar looking dwellings. The same builder had been contracted to build them all in a "one size fits all" kind of deal. They were cookie-cutter homes on a tract of land divided equally. Each plot provided for a living room, bedroom, dining area, kitchen, and a porch in the front, with a small backyard and front yard. An upper storey with a single room and bath next to the water tank was billeted. All units were tightly squeezed into a 400 square foot plot of land. An upgrade of a tile here or a closet there was offered for an additional negotiated price. It would be a few years before the municipality, after many requests and appeals, as well as a bribe to the official, would finally sanction a tar road. It took several more months for the street to be paved.

Mr. Agrawal bragged to his visitors that he had wangled a few more things from the contractor without paying an extra cent, like a ceiling fan for the dining room and an extra shelf in the living room and kitchen. In return, the contractor's son received a Java motorcycle at an employee discounted price.

"Quid pro quo," he bragged. His face lit up with an impish glee when he gloated that the house had appreciated 300 percent even before the mortgage was amortised.

The street had blossomed over the years with *Gulmohars*, *Badam* and *Neem* trees. With the lush foliage, it was pleasing to see such a fetching street of flowers. They provided much-needed shade from the blistering sun in summer, and the deluge in the rainy season. The *pipal* tree, with its thick foliage and dark green leaves by the house entrance, served as an air conditioner in summer by lowering the temperatures through evaporation.

The bougainvillea vine planted by his mother five years years earlier had grown quickly thanks to the sun rays falling on it. It climbed happily over the fence and gate with brilliant pink and magenta coloured flowers all the year around. Roop lifted the latch arm and parted the gate open. Its branches parted with it.

Mr. Agrawal worked as a sales executive in the Java motorcycle plant in the outskirts of the city. He worked his way up from a detailing boy to his current position of sales manager by hard work and initiative. He carried his medium build frame with energy and confidence and always looked spiffy in his starched and ironed whites with a company tie and logo. His job entailed marketing, promoting, answering queries, explaining new products and innovations, as well as overseeing the service department to ensure that customers were taken care of even after the vehicles were sold.

As a man without a specific job description, he did a bit of everything, switching between various roles seamlessly. He was accessible to anyone for anything that needed fixing. He was ubiquitous. He knew his product well. He was a master in explaining the efficiency of the vehicle, how many kilometres per litre of petrol, the pick up speeds, the power and torque, and how it surpassed its rival the Royal Enfield. He especially enjoyed explaining how the liquid cold engine generated higher speeds. This was a technical detail that he had read up on which required a fair amount of technical expertise.

Over the years, he had won several awards, including the coveted "most successful sales executive" of the region. He made himself indispensable, enjoying the kickback from customers for sweetening their deals on the side. His supervisor pretended not to notice and turned a blind eye as he met his sales targets, even exceeding them frequently. It was acknowledged that he was an overall asset to the company. In the fullness of time he earned the nickname "The Java Man." Mr. Agrawal's motto was "Get the job done with whatever it takes to get it done." His practise of having his palms greased by happy customers in return for service satisfaction took on an air of normalcy. It was a symbiotic arrangement.

While he was proud of his hard work and career advancement, he took nothing for granted. He knew only too well that everything could be upended in a moment of misfortune and bad luck. He never let his guard down.

Mrs. Agrawal was a simple lady who ran the house with thrift and efficiency. She was as wily as her husband and made sure that she got value for every rupee she spent in the domestic realm. She made sure that the servants earned their wages, and the vendors did not get the better of her in the day-to-day haggling and bartering of transactions. She managed the household frugally with every penny accounted for. Their daughter Kamini, five years older than Roop, was married to a young civil engineer in the hydro electric project. They gave the Agrawals two grandchildren who were the "apple of their eyes." They loved to babysit them when their daughter and son in law came to the city to see a movie.

The Agrawals had settled their daughter's alliance with a dowry of 25,000 rupees, the price tag attached to an eligible engineer at the time. However, the young couple actually received only five thousand rupees as the rest of the twenty was appropriated by the parents of the groom for the dowry needed in future to arrange the marriage of their daughter.

It was a "zero sum game" unless you had more boys than girls. The Agrawals were secretly delighted that Roop would pull in a higher dowry if he was successful in becoming a doctor. A dowry price of fifty thousand rupees was assigned by the marketplace for a newly minted doctor.

Roop was thus raised in a middle class ethos. Not too much or too little of anything but just the right quantity. Whether it was clothes or shoes or toys or anything at all of consequence. It was a mindset of moderation in all ventures and operations.

As Roop walked in, his mother, inquired, "Roop, how was your day? Did you walk home with Vir?"

"Yes, Mama."

"We have invited their parents tomorrow for tea." his mother informed him.

"Yes, Vir told me."

"Why don't you wash up? Your dad will be home soon."

"Okay."

Mrs. Agrawal, a slender lady in her thirties, was dressed in a traditionally embroidered blue saree with a silver border. She wore light makeup on a face that shone with dark brown eyes. The gleaming gold *mangalsutra*, the diamond drop earrings, and the gold bangles with floral motifs added modest opulence to her bearing. The ensemble was part of her wedding trousseau. She oozed a sense of cultivated importance. The "Home Minister" is how Mr. Agrawal humorously referred to his wife.

Soon the distinctive and loud sound of the Java motorcycle pulling into the gate heralded the arrival of Mr. Agrawal. Although he had a Fiat car, he preferred to ride the

Java, as it furthered his image of company loyalty. Besides, he figured that it would be more economical. Fuel prices had been rising with every budget of the finance minister. The family used the car only over the weekends to go to the temple or a movie or to visit family or friends. Mr. Agrawal drove the car himself. He could maybe afford a driver in a few more years, he figured.

With all three in tow, the family settled for dinner.

"So, what did you learn today?" asked Mr. Agrawal.

"The Razakar movement," replied Roop.

"Who gave the lesson?"

"Mr. Hussain."

"Oh, I see. How did he explain?" asked Mr. Agrawal.

"That Hindus were killed by Muslims and Muslims by Hindus."

"Hmm! I see," he said with a hint of suspicion in his tone.

"Did you take notes?"

"No, Mr. Hussain made notes for us. It gives the details of what happened."

"Let me look at it. I will also show it to the judge tomorrow," he added.

"Daddy, we are biking to Golconda fort on Sunday."

"Is Vir coming?"

"Yes."

"Is the judge ok with it?"

"Yes," Vir told me.

"Then it must be okay. I will have a look at your bicycle later."

"Thanks, Daddy."

The day thus ended for the Agrawals. It was an average sort of day.

CHAPTER 7

The Golconda Fort

If past is prologue
Does the future even exist?

The much-anticipated day arrived. It was a Sunday in March, a couple of weeks before the final exams which would seal their fates forever. The gang had planned and dreamed about it for months. It was much more than an interest in taking a peek at history. It was their first expedition. They would bike together to a treasure that was hidden away outside the city. The distance added further intrigue and excitement. It would test their endurance. The prospect of riding together made it less daunting. It inspired a sense of camaraderie and adventure to look forward to.

As the daytime temperatures rose to the nineties, they planned to leave early before the crack of dawn and ride back by dusk. The boys met at the bridge early in the morning. The sun had barely made it above the rooftops and the streets looked relatively empty. Compared to a weekday, Hyderabad was like a ghost town. A few fruit sellers were setting up their stalls while a drove of pigeons flew over the bridge flapping their wings.

The nearby mosque cast its shadow on the tranquil river below. In the distant horizon, the outline of the High Court and the Charminar was barely visible through the morning fog of the skyline. The colourful blossoms of hibiscus and poinsettias by the roadside added freshness to the morning scent.

The boys arrived at the appointed time of six and greeted each other with a hug. Prabu was there fifteen minutes earlier. He was the unofficially designated leader. They were there with their packed lunches and water bottles. The bikes were oiled and serviced for the journey. The handbells were tested for the "tring tring" sound. As promised, the judge had prepared a history summary of the Fort.

"You should read this to understand the history of the fort before you get there. I have made a copy for your friends," he had advised his son.

Vir distributed it to each of his friends at school the previous day. They had read it after reaching home. It was like a sneak preview before the actual movie.

The Judge's missive contained the following description:

"The fort city was built on a granite hill by the Kakatiya Dynasty around the thirteenth century. They were egalitarian and progressive in their outlook. They were Hindu rulers. They developed irrigation and a distinctive type of architecture. When their rule ended, the warrior class of the Nayakas united the clan against foreign invaders. There were wars between the Muslim and Hindu rulers over sovereignty. Finally, the fort fell to a Persianate Muslim empire.

Their rule gradually weakened, giving way to the Qutb Shahi dynasty in the late sixteenth century, which expanded the fort to its current size and shape. As their prosperity declined, the capital was shifted to the new city on the other side of the river. This was the new city of 'Baghnagar' or Garden City. Legend has it that the king built the new city to honour his beloved Hindu queen Bhagmati. It was later named Hyderabad.

The Golconda city had a booming economy. It produced high quality cotton and muslin that was exported to Persia and Europe. It was also a flourishing diamond trading centre. It produced the famous Kohinoor and Hope diamonds. The kohinoor is now part of the British Crown Jewels and the Hope Diamond is in the American Natural Museum.

There are four distinct forts with a long outer wall. There are eight gateways. There are a number of temples and mosques. A handclap below the dome at the entrance can be heard a kilometer away. This worked as a warning sign in case of an attack. The ornate peacocks and lions above the entrance door remind us of the fort's Hindu origins. The palaces and halls inside surrounded by beautiful gardens represent Mughal architecture. The fort symbolizes the conflicts and confluence of two religions and cultures."

John Keats, in his poem, *On Receiving a Curious Shell* refers to Golconda as "A gem, pure as an ice drop that froze on the mountain."

Prabu led the cycle beeline with Ramu, Roop, Patel, and Vas in the middle, and Vir bringing up the rear of the pack. They were on their way to make sense of the story the judge had prepared. Their ancestors might have been part of the stories. Unfortunately, they did not know their genealogy beyond their grandparents to make it personal.

Prabu set the pace, closely monitoring the progress of his friends behind him. He adjusted the mirror on the handlebar to capture their images. He pressed the bell trigger with his right thumb periodically to warn his friends of approaching rickshaws, scooters, and pedestrians. They progressed "in formation," like a gaggle of geese wading through a waterway in a straight line. He figured it would take about three hours to get there. They passed through narrow streets and unfamiliar villages as the traffic began to build.

He made the first stop after an hour, parking his bike along the huge trunk of a banyan tree. The others followed suit. Wetting his handkerchief with a few swishes of water, he wiped his face and downed some water from the flask. The sound of water was audible as it went down his throat in gulps. The others repeated the motions without exchanging a word.

Prabu announced that the next stop would be in an hour, near the police station when they would break for lunch. The rest nodded without questioning his decision. They knew that he knew what he was doing. It was a role he had grown into as the leader of the gang. With Prabu back in the saddle, the journey resumed.

Although it was a Sunday, he had to watch out especially for the morning commuters. Men and women who carried their livelihood in baskets balanced on their heads, and skinny men pulling oversized human specimens in rickshaws with sweat dripping down their faces. Their temple veins seemed to enlarge with every propulsion of the pedal. There were also the rich car owners who were chauffeured by barefooted drivers. They were likely being driven to their private clubs for a Sunday game of shuttle badminton or tennis.

As they advanced to the police station landmark, Prabu started slowing his bike and brought it to a halt under the *neem* tree next to the station. They wetted their faces and unwrapped the lunches packed by their mothers or servants in the wee hours of that morning. They took their time and relished the meal, sharing a bite or two with their mates.

After a half hour or so, Prabu motioned that it was time to leave. Holding his hands on the handlebars, he raised his right leg in a smooth arc to the pedal bar, anchoring the bike to the ground with his left foot. After a few jerky movements the bike steadied and began to pick up speed again. It was smooth sailing.

"Another hour and we will be there," he infomed as his friends came within earshot.

The bikes moved in synchrony until the fort began to appear in the distant horizon. As they inched their way forward the contours of the fort began to solidify. Finally, it was there right in front of them. The citadel was up close and humongous. The judge's description on paper came to life. There were the Peacocks and the Lions in the archway exactly as he had described.

Prabu entrusted the bikes to the boy in teens watching over the cycle stand. There were hundreds of them stacked against each other. He went over to the drink stall to buy ice cooled Fanta and the others followed. They downed it in quick gulps. It was refreshing and rejuvenating. Then Prabu went over to the counter to buy the entrance tickets. There was a reduced price of five rupees each, as they were students. He added up the amount mentally to settle the account later.

They were soon swamped by urchins selling postcards, women with babies in their arms begging for alms, and tour guides promising to show them the hidden wonders of the fort.

They settled with a young history student for a price of ten rupees. He began by explaining that it was called Golconda because it was *Gol,* or round, and *Konda*, meaning a hill.

"A round shaped hill," he asserted with a smile. He added there were 365 steps to reach the top. As he explained that it took over sixty years to build, he navigated them through the secret tunnels and escape routes, the private chambers, and the mosque with the five arches and Islamic lotus medallions. He pointed to the antique paintings, stone sculptures, swords, and shields. The vast inventory of Hindu and Muslim memorabilia were like envoys from another time and era. He enthralled them with the acoustic wonder of the "clap and whisper." Ramu's clap in the corner of the hallway could be heard a kilometre away. He also showed them the *Mahakali* Hindu temple, located in the midst of two rocks with its name written in both Hindi and Urdu. And so much more. They began to connect the Judge's notes with the visuals.

The Reunion

Ramu and Prabu realized how much the history of Hindus and Muslims was intertwined. They climbed to the top of the fort and looked down. It took their breath away.

The sun was beginning to set. The sky looked randomly orange and blue. The city below seemed hazy and its landmarks diminished. It was an old majestic city looking down on the sprawling new city below. The past looked at the present with the two connected archivally by a thread.

Ramu and Prabu thought about Rashid and Khazmi. Would the fort have reminded them of their ancestors? What questions would Mr. Hussain have posed today?

Patel stood alone admiring the scenery through his sunglasses. Roop and Vir had a quick look from the top and started their descent.

For a brief moment, it felt as if they were caught in a time warp that allowed images and stories from the past to have a conversation with the present. Would this day's memory remain with them?

It was time to ride home. The trek back seemed faster and shorter.

On the way home, they stopped by the rustic *Ganesh* temple on the roadside near the bus stop on jubilee hills road. Lodged in a small alcove, the deity of the Elephant God was painted red and anointed with oil and a marigold garland. The *diya* was lit with incense sticks emitting sandalwood fragrance. A young priest in a *dhoti* and vest was in charge. He performed a quick service for them.

The gang closed their eyes and held their hands together in prayer for success in the exams. The priest applied sandalwood *tilak* on their foreheads and held a silver platter in front of them with a burning camphor flame. They cupped their palms on it and withdrew it quickly to cover their faces with its warmth. Then they emptied their pockets on the platter. The coins dispersed with a scattering jingle.

Was this a new beginning for the young travellers in time? Time would tell.

They then rode away into the evening dusk.

CHAPTER 8
The Exams

When all is said and done
Are we by passage of time undone?

The month of March in 1964 was very hot in Hyderabad. The temperatures averaged in the mid nineties with warm air circulating in the atmosphere. The sky was overcast at times with only a thirty percent chance of rain. The days seemed longer with the sun rising around five in the morning and setting at about six in the evening. Muggy days were followed by muggy nights. People perspired copiously with ceiling and table fans rotating around the clock. Vendors exposed to the elements doused water on their faces to avoid a heatstroke while businesses and store owners cooled themselves with air conditioners. The *tamarind* tree near Vas's house provided refuge to hawkers, while the banyan tree in the old city near Rashid's house gave shade to worshippers kneeling for the midday prayer.

Families escaped to the parks in the evenings to seek respite from the blazing sun. While children ran around in the park enjoying the rides, parents sat on park benches under bushes and trees to watch over them. Lilies, daffodils, carnations, and roses bloomed in defiance of the hostile elements. The Public Gardens became a popular walking destination for couples either first thing in the morning or after sunset in the evening.

The six boys woke up in the wee hours to put their shoulders to the wheel. They memorized the study guides, lecture notes, and practise exam questions and answers that they had studiously collated in the months leading to the exam.

Babu attended the garden in the judge's villa. He watered it in the evenings. An earthy smell wafted through the air when the water made first contact with the soil. The daffodils and roses came back to life as their beds soaked up the water. The sun-beaten lawn began to perk.

The excavation on Abid's road, a busy commercial street, posed a hazard to commuters as the repairs proceeded at snail's pace. The heavy downpour had deepened the cavernous opening, blocking off the access to Roop's house. Mr. Agrawal had to ride his Java motorbike deftly around it, maneuvering his vehicle between the construction workers and the mounds of cement and shovels. He reached home in a foul mood, complaining, "The damn road has been in repair for nearly two months without any end in sight!"

When he telephoned the traffic department of the city to complain, the official on the line replied, "Sir, we are doing our best. We have assigned a couple of extra police to direct the traffic."

The boys gathered in the evenings at the tank bund park on Hussain Sagar Lake to study. It was a walker's paradise. The long promenade allowed one to have an uninterrupted

The Reunion

half hour walk each way. Young lovers sat on the benches, gazing at the lake while vehicles zipped on the road behind them. The red granite monolith of Buddha on the Gibraltar Rock in the lake towered above the horizon. The film star chief minister of the state had gotten the idea from the Statue of Liberty in New York.

The boys exchanged notes, discussed the answers, and quizzed each other. Prabu, Ramu, and Roop huddled for the biology part of the revision while Vas and Vir stepped to the corner for the math part. Patel floated between the two camps.

The exam date was set for two days in March. It would seal their fates forever. If things went as planned, there would be three doctors, two engineers, and one businessman. When the day arrived, they were in a sanguine mood. They were hopeful that with some luck their hard work would pay off. Failing was not an option as so much was at stake. If they did well in the exams, they could enjoy the summer holidays before embarking on their chosen paths.

Although they had studied together, their mode of final rehearsal was unique to each. Prabu and Ramu kept their notes short and simple, while Vas relied on longer summaries. Roop highlighted the main points with a blue crayon, while Vir just focused on practice questions and answers from previous exams. Patel was different from the rest. He seemed the most relaxed of all. After all, the outcome of the exam was not going to alter his future. It was a foregone conclusion that he would join the family jewelry business. It had been predestined by Kantibhai, the patriarch of the family.

As they parted company at the tank bund before the big day, there was a sense of nervous anticipation.

How would it all turn out? What would become of them? Would they remain friends after the exams? were some of the thoughts that crossed their minds.

The fathers counseled them in unique ways as well!

The judge advised Vir, "Get enough sleep. Go into the exam with a fresh mind."

Vas's father said, "Eat a light meal in the evening and a good breakfast tomorrow. Read the questions carefully before you answer."

Patel's dad: "You have read enough. Go for a movie in the evening. This will break the tedium of the exam."

Ramu's dad told him "Get up in the morning early and revise your notes one final time."

Roop's dad cautioned, "Leave enough time at the end to go over your answers."

All the mothers performed a special service in the temple on behalf of their sons.

Rashid's dad encouraged calm and blessed him. His mother gave him a lucky charm of a nickel pendant with "*Allah O Akbar*" inscribed on it. She prayed for his success at the nearby mosque.

Then, the exam day arrived. Everyone performed as expected. There were no surprises. They enjoyed the summer break meeting often, going to movies, playing cricket, visiting each others' homes, and visiting family and friends. The results were posted a month later.

Ramu, Roop and Prabu qualified for different medical schools. Vir and Vas received admission to engineering colleges, one in the city and the other in the district. Patel went to the Nizam College in Hyderabad for a Bachelor's degree in commerce. Rashid was selected for the Agricultural University in Hyderabad.

They said their goodbyes and promised to stay in touch. They did so for a few months. Then they moved to different places and their separate ways, making new friends and developing new interests.

A chapter had ended and a new one had begun. They thought of each other frequently and hoped to meet again sometime somewhere.

With Rashid, the relationship would be different. Like the metallic spring of a watch strap, it was extendable as needed, but returning always to a fixed constant.

Would the bonds they forged in school endure over time?

FIFTY-FIVE YEARS LATER

CHAPTER 9
The Java Man's Son

The bell that rang in a bygone time
Can only be re-rung by recalling the chime

Georgia, USA February 2019

Roop arrived in the USA in the seventies. After finishing medical school and internship in Hyderabad, his eyes were set on emigrating to the USA. He had heard that it was the land of milk and honey. Where dreams came true. Where he would become wealthy, own a big house, have two cars, send his children to private schools, and live the good life. His father, the Java Man, was totally supportive of this plan. He hoped Roop would not have to slave like him to afford the basic amenities of life.

There was no future for a young doctor in Hyderabad. A government doctor did not make much money and private practise was fiercely competitive. Homeopaths and mystic healers competed with doctors in the art of healing and even outdid them.

Their older daughter, Kamini, was now happily married, and Mr. Agrawal figured that if Roop could go to the USA, their family prestige would go up. They could hold their heads high in the community. He would be regarded as an important man with a foreign connection. He encouraged Roop to take the American qualifying exam in Singapore. He considered this a sound investment that would pay him back in spades. They were delighted when Roop passed the exam. He threw a party and invited his friends and family to celebrate his son's success. Before he left for America, he published his photo in the Deccan Chronicle with the caption, "Off to USA. Bon Voyage to Dr. Roop Agrawal."

Roop arrived in Atlanta to do his residency in 1971. He met Madhuri at a social event in the temple. She was also a fresh graduate who had arrived recently from Bombay to pursue her training in medicine. He plucked up courage to introduce himself to her in the temple dining hall. She was sitting by herself. She told him that she had to fight hard for permission to come abroad.

It was unusual for parents to allow girls to travel alone, especially to a foreign land. The community regarded this as a sign of modernity that was fraught with danger. Girls were at risk of being violated. Roop admired her courage and fell in love. They had much in common.

Both were new to the country and relied on each other for support as they navigated their careers. They met regularly and developed a relationship. He loved her beauty and confidence, and she admired his focus and reliability. They informed their parents of their intention to marry and both sets of parents endorsed it wholeheartedly. Madhuri's parents were especially pleased that Roop was a doctor from the same community.

The Reunion

They were married in Bombay at the end of their residency. The Agrawals held a reception in Hyderabad. Nearly five hundred guests attended, including colleagues from the Java dealership, friends from the neighborhood, relatives, and a few business associates who had helped him at critical points in his career. This was his way of saying "thank you."

Among the distinguished guests to attend were the CEO of the Java Company and the judge. Roop invited Vas, who was the only one left in Hyderabad. All the others had left to go abroad. They couldn't contact Rashid, as he was transferred to the districts as a government food scientist.

The judge informed Roop that Vir was doing well in the USA, working as an engineer in Michigan after completing his master's degree. He encouraged him to get in touch with him. He advised that childhood friendships were precious and should never be forgotten.

The young couple returned to the USA with the blessings of family and friends. Roop completed his fellowship in cardiology and joined a cardiology practice in Marietta, Georgia. Madhuri worked as an internist in the local hospital. After years of hard work, they had "arrived," so to speak. They were well positioned to pursue the American Dream. They moved to the suburbs and bought a huge house in Cobb County. Their two boys, Arun and Anoop, arrived in quick succession and excelled in school and college.

The county where they made their home was rooted in the history of the deep south. It was a rural borough with cotton plantations. These plantations, now a tourist attraction, were a reminder of the history of slavery in the past. Some places resembled scenes from the hit movie "Gone with the Wind." The characters and themes of the movie reminded one of how the genteels built their fortunes on the backs of the slaves. One could still visualize them toiling in the midday sun picking cotton while their white masters sat in the shade with fancy hats. One could see the remains of their quarters scattered around the plantation on the edges of the field.

The county was a sleepy suburb with a community of devout Christians who believed in law and order. They were socially conservative evangelical Christians who were predominantly white. The area had earned the nickname "Bible Belt" for their uncritical allegiance to the word of the Bible. The African American population lived in segregated areas with separate schools, libraries, and churches.

People from Atlanta started moving to the county in the last few decades to take advantage of high-end homes for half the price. It was a perfect place to retire in a "safe community," Roop stressed.

This was a republican stronghold that promoted Christian values, low taxes, controlled immigration, free market capitalism, gun rights, and a pro-life ideology. It was a package of sorts.

Roop and Madhuri embraced this narrative and invested in it. The Christian element of the package did not bother them as they kept their own faith in the Hindu temple. It was a fair trade-off for the luxurious lifestyle and status they enjoyed in the small community. Being a doctor helped Roop's station, as Indian doctors were now a "brand name," having gained recognition from the locals for their hard work and clinical acumen.

After trying unsuccessfully a couple of times for membership of the private country club, he finally got in, thanks to the recommendation of his senior partner. He would be one of only two non-white members to make the cut. His partner had to vouch for his character and standing in the medical profession.

When his cynical Indian friends questioned him of his modus operandi, Roop argued, "Well there is worse discrimination in India too, so what's the difference?"

"Isn't discrimination based on colour and race worse?" retorted one of them.

To which Roop replied, "Well the caste system in India is just as bad. In fact, it is worse."

He joined the Republican Party and eventually bought an even bigger five-bedroom house on a ten thousand square feet plot of land. There were doctors all around him. It came to be known as "Pill Hill." It was an exclusive piece of real estate. He was now a millionaire many times over. He had realized his father's dream. His social life was impressive. He played golf in the country club, while Madhuri joined the ladies' golf league. Like his neighbours, he proudly hoisted the American flag on his front porch. For all intents and purposes, he was no different from them. He enjoyed the same benefits as them. Although he had made a few good white friends, he still relied on the Indian community for social company.

The Indian community regarded him highly, consulted him on health matters, and extolled his professional accomplishments. They engraved his name on the Benefactors Wall in the temple for his generous fifty thousand dollar donation. He had negotiated his rightful place in both the white and Indian communities: a perfect balancing act. He straddled both identities with ease.

To add to their success, both their boys, Arun and Anoop, followed in their footsteps and became doctors. Arun married Melanie, a girl born and raised in the same county in a middle-class, churchgoing family. The couple met each other in a community fundraising event to help the war veterans of Iraq and Afghanistan. They moved to New York to pursue their careers and raise their two children. Arun, like his father, did a fellowship in cardiology at the Columbia teaching hospital in New York and settled in Westchester county. Anoop, their second son, specialized in oncology and moved to San Francisco. He was "an eligible but hardly interested in marriage" bachelor. Roop and Madhuri lamented that he showed little interest in meeting girls. They tried every which way to hook him up, advertising in the Indian newsletters, exploring suitable matches in the Indian community, and even talking to friends in India for prospective brides. Their proposals were met with unwavering refusal!

Both their children left the county bubble, moving from rural to urban, and from conservative to progressive areas. They were clearly at odds with the values they had been raised with. They were even voting for the Democratic Party!

As Roop and Madhuri prepared for the reunion, spring arrived in Georgia. The red, yellow, and pink flowers in their garden replaced the weary blues of winter. The parks and trails came alive. Birdwatchers were out with their binoculars to spot seabirds and bobcats. The election fever was beginning to rise along with the temperature.

Roop and his friend Jim organized a fundraiser for the republican senatorial candidate. They had voted for Trump in 2016 and would do so again in 2020. They were convinced that he was what America needed. "Policies are more important than Character," was their chant and mantra. The anti-immigrant rhetoric and Muslim ban appealed to Roop. This was his reason to support Modi as well. The politics in America and India seemed to intersect. He was convinced that the democratic party had been taken over by socialists who would raise taxes and take away their Cadillac health care insurance plan. They were also concerned that the country would be flooded with Chinese goods.

Roop and Madhuri were eager and excited about the reunion in Michigan. But for an occasional phone call with Vir, he had lost touch with the rest of the gang. The conference call ignited the urge to meet, to see how everyone was, what they had done with their lives, if they had made money, how their children had done, and if they were successful doctors and lawyers. The curiosity was endless. He was also eager to share his success with them.

Madhuri booked their flight in business class for the July fourth reunion. She started planning what she would wear and what jewelry, handbag, and footwear would match with which outfit. She had blossomed into an elegant sixty-five-year-old woman. Although she had gained a little weight lately due to hormonal issues, and her facial skin looked a little coarse, she was always immaculately dressed, wearing clothes from Bloomingdales or Nordstroms. It was a practise refined over the years by keeping up with the ladies of the club.

Roop had grown into a somewhat obese seventy-year-old with a prominent midriff. The face he saw in the mirror reminded him of his father. The patriarchal resemblence once a source of curiosity was now a matter of pride and comfort. He was even-tempered with a soft voice and a slight frown on his face. His sparse black hair was combed over the scalp prudently to hide the barren patches. A quiet confidence had replaced the timid and shy demeanour of youth.

His father had died of a heart attack in Hyderabad the previous year. Roop went home to perform the final funeral ceremonies. The Java colleagues attended the "tenth day ceremony" of the mourning period. They recalled his energy and zeal in pitching the perfect tone to sell bikes. They were nostalgic over his loyalty to the company. He had become somewhat of a "folk legend" due to his wily ways of winning colleagues and customers over.

He learned from his mother that the judge had passed away. Vir had come home to do the final rites. The newspapers had chronicled his career from "Advocate to Chief Justice" as an important chapter in Hyderabad jurisprudence. The headline was "Passing of an Era."

Roop's father's life and times was now an integral part of who he was. His hard work, ambition, and recognizing the value of money and family in achieving "status and happiness" was now part of his own life narrative.

He was glad that his parents had visited him just five years ago, remembering how much his dad enjoyed going to

The Reunion

the country club and being introduced to "foreigners," as he would call his friends. He thought the world of his son and enjoyed being driven in his Mercedes. It was a far cry from his tiny Fiat car in India.

His mother decided to move in with his sister after his dad's passing, and Roop deposited two hundred dollars a month in her account for her expenses and upkeep. He could not find the time to look up Vas or Rashid. Besides, it was a short visit and he did not even know where or how to find them.

When he boarded the flight back to Atlanta after the ceremonies in India, it felt like he was returning home. Hyderabad was now fading as a memory. His connection was tenuous. It was a past that he no longer felt tethered to.

Perhaps the reunion might bring it back to life?

CHAPTER 10

The Judge's Scion

A prodigal son
Was once his father's son!

Michigan, USA February 2019

Vir came to the USA in the seventies after completing his bachelor's degree in mechanical engineering at the university in Hyderabad. The judge was excited about his son's achievement although he secretly bemoaned that he had not taken up law. Vir, always independently minded, pursued his own calling rather than succumb to family pressures to succeed the judge. Besides, the judge was a tough act to follow. Having set his sights on the USA from high school, he applied for admission to a master's program at the University of Michigan.

After a few months of anxious waiting, the envelope arrived with the good news. A scholarship awaited him in Ann Arbor, a well recognized publicly funded Ivy League university about fifty kilometres from Detroit.

Ambitious and eager to chart his own course, he began to prepare for the trip. The judge bought him a samsonite suitcase and fitted him with two woolen suits at Raymond's on Abid road. He had researched about the cold winters in Michigan. A winter coat was purchased from a dealer who imported winter clothing from the cold state of Kashmir. He took him to the Bata Store for waterproofed leather shoes as well as bathroom slippers..

As the government only sanctioned twenty dollars for foreign travellers, Mrs Srivastava begged the judge to do something. She could not bear the thought of her son starving for a meal in a foreign country. Finally, he gave in to his wife's pressure and finagled foreign currency of hundred USA dollars from one of his contacts who made frequent trips abroad. He settled by paying him the equivalent amount in rupees. This was antithetical to everything he stood for. He carried this on his conscience. His wife was relieved that this would see her son through until he received the first check of the university scholarship. At the last minute, she tucked some sweets and pickles in the side pouches of the bulging suitcase. She had heard that food was very bland overseas as they did not add any hot spices to the cooking.

The judge's secretary prepared a brown luggage tag with his name and new address in America printed in bold black letters. The labels were slapped on the front and back of the suitcase and secured with office glue. Mrs. Srivastava finally tied a pink ribbon bow to the suitcase handle for easy identification.

The parents flew with him to Bombay to see him off. Before his final goodbye, the judge advised, "Work hard. Be honest. Follow the rules."

The Reunion

Tearing up, his mother pleaded, "Be safe. Don't drink. Don't smoke."

And then he was away on the most interesting expedition of his life. He settled in the campus quickly and learned the ropes of "foreign student life" within a matter of weeks. He learned where to eat cheaply, and how to use public transportation with low fares, borrow books by placing strategic holds in the library, and save on groceries by collecting coupons. He crashed at the Hindu temple for a free meal on weekends.

Vir adapted to the new climate and country and made new friends and connections. He studied hard as per his father's advice and aced in all his courses. He graduated with honours.

Then Vir applied for a job in an electrical cable company in Detroit. A few years went by before he was promoted to middle level management. His initiative and enterprise as well as interpersonal and networking skills caught everyone's attention. His boss predicted that he was destined to succeed and rise to higher echelons of management. As an eligible sought-after bachelor with foreign credentials and a good job, he was now a "desirable catch" in the matrimonial market as well.

The judge had already arranged an alliance with Meena, the daughter of an IAS officer, Mr. Khanna, whom he knew well. It was a "match made in heaven," he announced. Vir went to India to seal the deal. The couple were introduced to each other briefly when they exchanged a few pleasantries. Vir had full confidence that his father would have considered all factors before recommending the match. He agreed to the match without reservation.

Meena had just completed her BA at the Women's College. She was attractive and confident, traits that Vir valued and liked. A grand wedding was arranged in the newly built banquet hall in the city. Prominent lawyers and government officials as well as the governor and chief minister of the state attended the ceremony and reception. The couple received gifts in spite of the judge's refrain on the card that blessings would suffice.

Vir had invited his buddy Vas and his young wife Savitri to the wedding. They too had tied the knot a year ago. He located them among the guests and chatted for a while. They promised to keep in touch. Rashid was contacted at the last minute, but could not attend as he was a few hundred miles away in the district and could not come in time for the wedding. He sent his apologies through Vas.

Vir took his new bride to Ooty, a hill station in the south, for their honeymoon. Ooty was a resort that the Brits used for their summer sojourns. The temperate climate was a welcome relief from the heat and humidity of Hyderabad. The couple enjoyed the halcyon quality of the place to get to know each other. Vir was proactive in initiating the paperwork for her visa and promised her that it would be less than six months before she would join him.

Vir returned to the USA as a married man. His wife joined him as planned. They made their first home in a duplex in Ann Arbor. Their daughter, Preeti, arrived a year after that. Restless with ambition, Vir applied for a senior management position in the county in a packaging factory.

Within a couple of years of joining, an opportunity to buy a fledgling chemical engineering plant presented itself. Hazarding a risk, he seized the opportunity, and applied for a loan to become the sole owner of the company. Working day and night, he turned its fortune around.

Before long, a hundred employees were working for him. His business boomed and his assets grew. His bank manager gave him special perks as a high net-worth individual. He didn't have to wait in line for a teller, as the manager attended to him personally. He chatted with him at the club as well to inform him of new products. A private wealth manager came home to discuss investments. He didn't miss out on any opportunity. The largesse bestowed a lifestyle that was exclusive to the rich and famous. He was now a multi-millionaire.

Meena was as ambitious as Vir. She prevailed on him to buy a mansion with six bedrooms in a wealthy enclave of the county. It was a rich and exclusive enclave with its own security detail, reinforced with the latest technology. They could monitor their home even when they were thousands of miles away on vacation. It was a safe place to raise their daughter. The small town had grown on Meena over the years. She knew it well.

Unlike Detroit, it was easy to navigate and get around, traffic was usually manageable, and parking was never an issue. She hardly ever used the GPS as she knew the town like the back of her hand. She loved to explain to their "out of town and out of country" visitors that the county with a population of around 150,000 was the "most liveable place" in the world. It was named after James Monroe, the fifth president. She also took them downtown and showed them the statue of George Custer, the commander in the American civil war. Although the town was initially known for its paper mills, there were now coal firing and nuclear generating plants and other industries.

"The temperatures are moderate," she would add, "neither too hot nor too cold." They were among the ten percent of minorities in the county. The rest of the ninety percent was white.

It was considered a swing county which voted for Trump in 2016. Vir's was one of the fifty "well to do" families from India who voted for him. There were also a large number of Indian families who did not vote for him. They feared that he was using them for his own gains and that their children and grandchildren would be subject to attacks by the white supremacists who he covertly courted. The two groups locked horns frequently, which resulted in flaming arguments. They finally settled for a truce. To agree to disagree without being disagreeable.

Their daughter, Preeti, married a doctor from the same town. They had attended the same school. They had two children who were doted on by their grandparents. They moved to Lansing so that he could work in a teaching hospital. He built a thriving practise and bought a lovely home in the rich suburbs. They sent their kids to a private school.

Like her mother, Preeti supported her husband in building his image. She was an active member of the ladies' group in the golf and country club. The young family made it a point to have dinner every Friday night at the club. Over the weekends, they drove to visit his or her parents in

Grand Rapids. They were a young family experiencing the American dream just as their parents had! In fact, they felt more American, as they were born here.

Preeti's in-laws had emigrated from Eastern Europe. They felt that they belonged. Unlike their parents, they felt conflicted when the republican campaign touted slogans of "Make America Great Again." They were confused as they were not sure what it meant. They could not identify with it. They felt that they were part of an America that was already great. Preeti wasn't sure why her dad was even wearing the red hat!

Vir retired at the age of sixty-five with an annual income of five hundred thousand dollars. This was in addition to the social security check and Medicare health benefits that he joked were "Socialist perks" that he could do without.

Vir was now tall and gangly, with intense eyes and a receding hairline, and there was a sense of purpose to everything he did. There was a hesitancy to his walk, with a slight droop due to arthritis of the knee.

He was a man who had achieved what he had set out to achieve. He was secure and self assured. Now he was transitioning into the evening of his life with deep pockets. He maintained the membership of the country club and played tennis, but only a single set of doubles. The days of singles were over. He got involved in local and national politics and became a card-carrying member of the republican party. He contributed to the political campaign and voted for Trump in 2016. He admired his call for patriotism, the "buy America" slogan in particular, ban of Muslims, and tariffs on

Chinese goods. He forbade his wife from buying anything Chinese, not even a toothbrush or a tube of toothpaste.

Vir was going to support Trump again in 2020. He joined the "Hindus for Trump" campaign and corralled others in the temple to raise funds. He was convinced that America would become a socialist country if the democrats came to power. His hard-earned assets would diminish.

He informed Meena about hosting the reunion in July. She was excited. She began to plan for their guests. She said she would have the Taj Restaurant cater the meals. She would hire their waiters to serve. One meal they would have at the club. Meena reminded Vir to tell his friends, especially Vas from India, to bring a jacket and tie for the club dinner, as they strictly enforced the dress code. They would drive them to the Ford Museum in Detroit and, time permitting, they would plan a trip to Niagara Falls. Meena said a visit to the temple was a must as she wanted to show the new dining hall that they had donated for.

Vir often thought of the comment made by his father about his mansion. They had visited them some years ago. The judge compared their house to a "golden cage." Quite luxurious, but too quiet for their liking. They missed the buzz and hullabaloo of Hyderabad and the sights, sounds and smells of their neighborhood. Vir hoped that his school friends, especially Vas from Hyderabad, would not feel so stifled.

"By the way, the agent called me about the cottage in Florida," Vir told Meena.

"We should wrap it up," she replied.

The Reunion

The bitter cold winters were becoming intolerable. They didn't want to spend another winter in Michigan.

"Do you miss your classmates?" she asked.

"Yes, sometimes," he said. The conference call had infused in him a sense of excitement.

Although he was retired, he kept a close eye on the market and called his broker at least once a week to buy this or sell that. He had become active in the re-election campaign of the local congressman. He had a picture taken with him which he displayed in the family room. He was yearning for a photo with Trump and learned that it would cost him ten thousand dollars. He was eager to buy the privilege.

He chatted often with his neighbor Jim across the hedge and loved repeating the mantra "We shouldn't let the socialists get in."

His other neighbor Ed, an evangelical Christian, moaned, "Our country is in trouble if people abandon their faith and allow liberals to corrupt our morals." He was confident that Trump was their best hope to preserve Christian values.

Vir agreed and said Hindus in India were also fighting for traditional Hindu values. He said young college girls in India had lost their "moral compass" and needed to be tempered. "BJP and Modi," he said, "are the last best Hope for India."

This resonated with his Christian friends.

In his moments of reflection, he wondered what his dad might have thought of him, if he would be proud of his financial success and standing in the community. This was usually a passing thought. After all, he rationalized, he belonged to another time and place.

Meena seemed ensconced in her role as Vir's wife. She got along famously with the ladies of the club. She did not feel any incongruence in conforming to the "Family Values" morals of a small county town.

CHAPTER 11

Like Father, Like Son

That happiness is a choice
May take a lifetime to realize

Toronto, Canada February 2019

Like his classmates, Ramu came to North America and settled in Canada in the Seventies. He was now almost bald with a medium build, and wore a perpetually serene face with dark brown eyes and ears sticking out like handles. He had been in Toronto with his wife Padmini since his arrival in Canada.

They saw Toronto grow over the years from a predominantly "white city" in the seventies to the most multicultural city in the world. The BBC and the United Nations hailed it as the most diverse city on the planet. They were now among more than half the residents of the city who were born outside Canada. Ramu liked to call himself a "Torontonian" and felt it was his "home away from home." Actually, it was his only home since his parents passed away in India.

There was a ten-year age difference between Padmini and himself which became physically less apparent as they got older. Upon graduation from medical school in Hyderabad, Ramu had hoped to get a seat in internal medicine for his post graduate studies, but he was unsuccessful. He fell just short of the marks required in the open competition and did not qualify for any of the quotas reserved for students from remote districts and other reservation categories. He was not interested in the USA or the UK as he had heard about the racial tensions in the two countries in the seventies.

Canada was a default option. He had read about Pierre Trudeau, the charismatic prime minister at the time and his policy of "Multiculturalism" inviting immigrants from South Asia to apply. Ramu was also tickled by the "Trudeaumania" that was gripping the country at the time with his youthfulness and promise of bringing change. He applied for a visa and received it within a month. However, he had no job and took the huge risk of emigrating without one. He hoped to find one soon in this sparsely populated "great white country of opportunities in the north."

He looked up the map and settled on the most populated capital city of Toronto. He had read that the weather in Toronto was similar to North American cities like New York and Chicago with very warm summers and very cold winters.

He and Padmini were married in India before Ramu left for Canada. The two families knew each other well, and Padmini's father convinced her mother that the advantages of the alliance outweighed the age difference.

"Ramu belongs to a respectable Brahmin family," he told her. He made discreet inquiries of Ramu's habits and prospects and concluded that the "boy is of good character."

Padmini had barely turned eighteen when the marriage took place. She had only completed high school and her dreams of going to college were dashed. This would become a lifelong lament for her. The disappointment was somewhat assuaged a few years later when she earned a degree in accounting from the polytechnic in Toronto and landed a job in a non-profit organization that helped children from low income families with scholarship funds. The family was proud of her work and sense of idealism. She was viewed as the moral guide to determine the right and wrong of day to day matters; she was a litmus test of sorts used to scrutinize their behaviours.

Upon arriving in Toronto in the month of January, Ramu was captivated by the sleek and shiny airport with marbled walls and carpeted floors. The baggage area was quiet and organized. No one scrambled for his or her suitcase as he had seen in Bombay. Everyone waited patiently for it.

They were greeted cordially by the immigration officer. After checking the documents, he said, "Welcome to Canada," with a smile.

This greeting would become a permanent memory. Ramu often recalled it nostalgically.

The city was icy cold on the day of their arrival. As the taxi drove them through downtown to their motel, he had a glimpse of the towering CN Tower. It hovered over the tall buildings, narrow streets, yellow taxis, and streetcars. Its magnificent obelisk with the space needle piercing the sky was a sight to behold.

Within a week of arriving, Ramu managed to get an interview at the Mount Sinai hospital for a spot in the residency program. The interview went well, and he was offered a position. They were surprised that he could speak in grammatically correct English in spite of his accent. The job came with subsidized accommodation.

They soon met other Indians and discovered the Indian grocery stores and restaurants on Gerrard Street. The temple became the "meeting point" where they found out where to shop and which schools to send their children. They were quite excited when they ran into someone from Hyderabad and struck up a conversation instantly with them. Some would later become their close friends.

Ramu completed his training and became a radiologist at the Toronto General Hospital. His son, Rishi, and daughter, Mina, were born within two years of each other. They attended the neighborhood schools. Rishi excelled in his studies in college and went to Stanford to do Law. He met Susan, an Irish girl in law school there, and married her. Susan worked as an immigration counselor for recently arrived refugees. They had two children.

Ramu's daughter, Mina, married Ram, a software engineer and moved to Chicago after her marriage. They had a daughter who had just turned two.

As Ramu progressed in his profession, he and Padmini bought a home in Cherry Hill, a fairly affluent suburb in Toronto. The Gopalans, his parents, visited them from India a couple of times. They enjoyed the clean surroundings and the parks around his house. The suburb was elevated above the other counties of Toronto. Their house was a detached three bedroom on a cul-de-sac with a garden and easy access to the subway. Padmini loved gardening and created an idyllic space where the two of them spent many evenings in spring and summer. She took great pride in the hanging planters, the splash of flower colours, the manicured lawn, and the pine and maple trees that had matured with them over the years. She especially loved to sit by herself on the white stone slab and read to the cooing sounds of pigeons and doves. The garden was her sanctum. Their house had morphed into a home.

They were a part of a fast growing and prosperous community with successful immigrants from India and China. A local repertory presented good plays. Ramu and Padmini subscribed to the season membership and looked forward to the shows on Saturdays. The newly built mall had all the stores they needed. It was a "self contained community," as Ramu described it. He had taken up golf in his later years and enjoyed playing in the public courses with his colleagues and friends. The discounted "senior green fees" was an additional perk that added thrill to the rounds.

Ramu retired with a decent pension and modest gains from his blue-chip stock investments. The returns were dependable. He preferred to describe himself as a "risk-averse and safe investor." He was much like his own father, years ago, who deposited small amounts into the interest earning savings account regularly. His retired lifestyle was predictable. He got up early, had a morning cup of freshly brewed coffee, walked to Tim Hortons to shoot the breeze with friends, read history and biographies, and entertained friends.

He had been sleeping well now for years. The awful and frightening dreams from his dreadful encounter with Mr.Jeevan, his private math tutor at the age of seven became less frequent and gradually faded away. Was it just the passage of time or had he gotten the better of it? He wasn't sure.

His mother passed away after a brief illness, and Mr. Gopalan moved into a retirement community in Coimbatore, a town about 500 kilometres from Chennai. He preferred this, as it offered South Indian vegetarian food and a culture he was accustomed to. He was especially glad of the laundry and housekeeping amenities, a doctor on twenty-four-hour call, an ambulance on premises, and a clubhouse where he could interact, play cards, and converse with like-minded residents. Ramu made a point of visiting him once a year to spend time with him and take him to Hyderabad to meet his sister, Ramani, and his old university colleagues. Finally, he succumbed to a viral infection. He was sick for a couple of weeks and gradually slipped away. He died "as simply as he lived," Ramu would remember, with his eyes turning misty. He kept in touch with his sister Ramani by a weekly phone call.

They looked forward to the visits of their children in summer. The grands enjoyed the garden as well as the entertainment parks and activities in the vicinity. They were very pleased that their son and daughter were close to each other. Their daughter-in-law, Susan, had integrated well into their family, and everyone loved her.

The Reunion

"Life is beautiful," Ramu would often tell his friends.

He loved to discuss current affairs, and especially the upcoming elections in the USA. He feared that if Trump were re-elected, it would be unsafe for his grandchildren to be raised in the USA. He and his friends were also nervous that "white nationalism" might cross the border into Canada. The relative "peace, quiet, and safety" was deemed precious and needed to be preserved and protected at any cost.

Ramu told Padmini about the conference call and the reunion in July. He would be meeting his friends again after decades. Prabu from Vancouver and Vas from India would visit them first for a few days. They planned to drive together to Michigan. They wondered what gift to buy for Vir, as he was going to host them. Padmini wondered about a coffee table book on Toronto. Ramu told Padmini about Prabu's recent heart attack and that he was in rehab.

Padmini said she would call his wife Mohini in Vancouver to find out if he had any dietary restrictions.

"Let's call the kids," he said.

Ijust spoke to them," she replied.

"How is Susan?" he asked.

"She is taking some cooking lessons in South Indian food. The boys are in summer camp."

"What about Rishi?"

"He said, he is volunteering for the Biden campaign," she informed him.

Ramu nodded in agreement.

It would be another few months before Prabu and Vas would arrive. After reflecting upon this, Ramu and Padmini then settled down for a lunch of rice, beans curry, eggplant *sambar, rasam,* pickles, and *curd rice*. Ramu relished the meal and thanked his wife. The food, he told her, was "divine!"

He then looked out through the kitchen window. The ground was covered with snow. A man was walking his dog and a few kids were tobogganing on the tiny hill. The aspens and birches were showing signs of spring with sprouting of fresh leaves.

He grabbed his iPhone and took a picture. He sent it to his children with the caption "Spring is here after a long and harsh winter."

CHAPTER 12

The Jeweler Abroad

Is what we leave behind
Slowly let go with time?

Birmingham, U.K. February 2019

Patel, had been living in England now for about five decades, much longer than he had lived in India. He arrived in England in the early seventies. He completed his Bachelor of Commerce degree from Nizam College in Hyderabad. This was the minimum scholastic "right of passage" required of a young Patel to join the family jewelry business. Kantibhai, his uncle and patriarch of the family, was a high school graduate himself. He had insisted that the younger generation needed to do a little better, and have at least a bachelor's degree in commerce with a working knowledge of English, to function optimally in a fast-growing jewelry business that involved foreign travel and interaction with "white people."

Kantibhai travelled to London and the Middle East regularly to promote their new businesses outside India. They catered to Indians living abroad, as they still fancied twenty-two karat gold jewelry as part of the trousseau to daughters at the time of their weddings. There were also men who liked to wear bracelets and gold chains with religious symbols. It was a symbol of power and wealth in a foreign country. Kantibhai kept abreast of changing fashions by chatting with his managers abroad. Ornaments of pure gold and silver, he outlined, "cast a spell" by their sparkle. They "light a fire" in the hearts of young women. He imported western styles and designs to cater to modern women in India who loved to wear chic western jewelry to match their modern outfits. These were the anglicized "nouveau riche" with a schmaltz for "Good Old England."

Some of them had mixed ancestry with distant connections to the British. They regarded English as their mother tongue and resisted the imposition of Hindi to replace English. They talked and thought in English. Engelbert Humperdinck, the pop singer who was born in Madras, was claimed as one of their own. So was the English singer Cliff Richard, who was born in Lucknow. These were vanishing remains, it seemed, of a bygone age!

Kantibhai employed Mr Mistry, a *parsi* gentleman, to head their branch in London. He was westernized, lived and slept in a three-piece pinstripe suit, and spoke English like the English. He smoked a cigar and liked to end the day with a peg of single malt. He was a perfect ambassador to promote a *gujarati owned* business in a foreign land. Their store on Grosvenor Street flourished. He hoped that his nephew Patel would someday succeed Mistry. That moment arrived in 1971 when Mr. Mistry suffered a heart attack.

Patel, still in his mid-twenties, was anointed by Kantibhai as his successor to replace him.

A marriage was speedily arranged with Nalini, a girl from the *gujarati* community with a high school education. Her parents owned an electrical wholesale business that made a fortune. Their business was brisk. The community shopped there for anything from bulbs and fuse boxes to generators and transformers. They cornered the market. Kantibhai spoke to her father Haribhai, an old business acquaintance of his, and fixed the alliance. This was relayed to the other members of the joint family more as an "FYI" rather than to solicit an opinion. His parents accepted the decision without reservation. All the others followed. Chandu and Nalini were the last in the information chain to be informed. They agreed to the proposal without any ifs, ands or buts.

The wedding was conducted with about a thousand people in attendance. Vibrant colours, catchy folksy music, scrumptious vegetarian dishes, and fun wedding games marked the grand celebration. There was also the exchange of jewelry and dowry. Kantibhai negotiated the details. Finally, *Griha Shanti Pooja*, a ritual for the stars to align and give the couple a happy and peaceful married life, was performed. Nalini and her father broke down when it came to the *Kanyadaan* ceremony, the giving away of his daughter to the groom's family. The priest sealed the deal by tying the holy knot between Patel's shawl and the end of Nalini's luxuriant and magnificent red sari. It was draped sensuously around her hips and shoulders, gracefully covering her midriff and bosom. The couple looked picture-perfect. The wedding photographer captured the moment splendidly.

The memory would remain secure forever in a silver frame. It travelled with them on their first voyage to England.

Patel and Nalini would never forget the first time they set foot on English soil. It was a blustery cold October day. Mr. Mistry received them and took them to the two-bedroom flat he had rented. It was in the west end of London in Southall. Mr. Mistry sensed that they would feel "at home" in this town. A large Indian community settled there. There were Hindus, Muslims and Sikhs who lived in harmony. A Hindu temple, mosque, and gurdwara were the hub and heart of the community. Jewelry and grocery stores, restaurants, gas stations, cinema halls, travel agencies and other businesses had mushroomed in the last decade. They were all owned by immigrants. It would come to be widely known as "Little India."

Patel worked very hard and learned the new ways of conducting business from Mr. Mistry. He groomed him in social graces, nuances of the English language pertaining to accent and pronunciation, and use of common idioms. He introduced him to their English business associates and observed the interaction to correct blunders. Finally, after a couple of months of probation, he decided to leave him to his own devices. He was satisfied that Patel was ready and would grow into the role with time and experience. He then called it a day. Kantibhai travelled to England for his retirement party. He presented him with a pure silver plaque with his name and years of service engraved on it. He combined it with an adequate pension to sustain his English way of life.

After a few years in England, Patel felt like a shoo-in. He decided that there was potential to expand the business to the predominantly Indian areas of Birmingham, Leicester, and Bradford in the midlands. With Kantibhai's approval, he opened a new branch in Birmingham. He was tired of living in London and wanted to be part of a smaller Indian community. So, he and Nalini bought a place in Birmingham. They figured it would be the ideal place to settle and start a family.

They soon welcomed their son Harish to their new home in Birmingham. The business picked up with Patel commuting to London as well as managing the branch in Birmingham. Kantibhai, now elderly and frail, travelled to open new branches in Leicester and Bradford as well. They appointed managers from the *gujarati* community to run them. Patel directed them by phone as well as in person on his weekly visits. He was proud that the family business established a hundred years ago by his grandfather had blossomed into a "mini empire." He was also proud that he had played a pivotal role in its overseas operation. He attributed his success to the motto "Work hard, be positive, be happy" that Kantibhai had instilled.

His son, Harish, grew up in Birmingham and went to medical school, specialized in anaesthesia, and worked at the general hospital. Patel was secretly proud that his son was much more educated than him and had broken the "BCom mould," the standard bearer for his generation. Besides, in his opinion, a doctor was equal to "God Himself," as they decided matters of life and death. He was a little unsure, however, as to who would pick up the business mantle from him. Regrettably, it would end with him.

They celebrated the wedding of Harish with Jyoti who was also from the *gujarati* community. The wedding celebration was grand. He invited the local English MP, as well as the mayor to attend. They both did. The reception at the Sheraton was attended by 500 guests. This was to reciprocate the invitations they had received for weddings of their sons and daughters. The *barat* procession was colourful with Harish riding on a horse surrounded by dancing men and women to a musical band scoring old Hindi movie hits. The procession travelled through the busy downtown area to the marriage venue, as stunned white passersby looked on in awe.

The newly wedded couple began to build their life together. Their parents were an intrinsic part of their family life. Jyoti gave birth to a beautiful girl in the first year of their union. Patel and Nalini were delighted. They doted and thoroughly spoiled her. Daughter-in-law Jyoti was a kind and gentle girl who respected the Patels. She was raised to be deferential to them. In fact, she was raised to consider them as her second parents. And they treated her as a daughter. Their son advanced rapidly in his profession, thanks to hard work and an English boss who recognized his talents. England was in an economic downturn. The recession had wreaked havoc with high unemployment. The immigrants were blamed by the native born residents for taking jobs away . The economy picked up again after a winter of discontent. Patel's business recovered from the temporary downturn and the business boomed.

Looking back, living and raising his family in Birmingham in the seventies was a challenge for Patel.

There were IRA bombings, bomb scares, and racial tensions. Margaret Thatcher became the first woman Prime Minister. There were regular strikes in mines and industries. Bell- bottoms was a new fad. Enoch Powell became famous for his "Rivers of Blood" speech, also called "Birmingham Speech," criticizing the government on their liberal policy of immigration, especially of South Asians. This sent shivers through the Indian community.

Powell created a political storm when he became the chief spokesman for immigration control. The National Front, a far-right political party, reached new heights by playing on minds of electors about the growing concern over South Asian immigrants who arrived in droves from Uganda when Idi Amin expelled them, calling them "bloodsuckers." They came with nothing except a British passport in their hands. The residents feared that such an exodus would erode the English way of life.

In the midst of this turmoil, Patel carried on with life as usual. He brushed aside any fears that it would affect his family or business. His son sometimes came home scared, having been bullied at school with hateful taunts of "Paki go home."

Patel drew him close and advised, "Tell them you are not a Paki. Remind them they looted our country for 200 years." After a while, Harish stopped complaining to his father, as it made matters worse.

Patel thrived in Birmingham. He employed about fifty employees to service all the branches. He hired some English girls to "glamourise the showrooms." He also gave a break to several newly arrived immigrants from India and Uganda.

Now in his seventies, Patel had lost touch with his school gang. The last time they spoke was in high school. He often wondered where they might be. He was quite surprised when he got a call from Prabu, who had tracked him down through Vas, the only one in Hyderabad. Vas had traced him through his father at their store in the old city.

He told Nalini about the reunion in July. They called their travel agent who put together an itinerary that would cover Detroit, New York, and Washington D.C. Then they'd go to Florida to see Disney world. They were promised, as always, the best fares possible. The agent also applied for the Visas on their behalf.

Hotel bookings were made in *gujarati*-owned motels with guarantees of *gujarati* breakfasts consisting typically of *chai*, *dhokla*, *purées* with potato *subzi* and *jalebi* for dessert. They purchased Blue Cross insurance as they were warned that a visit to the emergency room would make a deep hole in their pocket or even bankrupt them!

Over the preceding few years Patel had developed diabetes and hypertension. He grew a generous belly that extended a foot and a half in front of him. Averse to any form of exercise, he was reckless in his food habits. He ate as he pleased. Often casually dressed, and silvery haired, his face carried a permanent smile. He was warm and affable in temperament, bearing the persona of one who is comfortable in his skin.

He and Nalini were quite involved in the community. They socialized with friends, spent time with their granddaughter, attended weddings, and enjoyed movies and songs. They visited India yearly. They blended into the culture there as if they had never left India. Both his father and Kantibhai passed away in short order, leaving the youngest uncle to take on the reins of the family. His mother and the matriarch aunt continued to live under the same joint family roof after losing their spouses. His older cousin, Dilip, was groomed to replace Kantibhai. The business in India was prosperous.

His doctor son advised him often of the risks of heart disease, but it usually fell on deaf ears. Patel walked with his nose in the air when his son became the chief of anaesthesia in the local hospital.

"Things have changed in England," he said. "Indian doctors are now preferred over other nationalities. If I had worked hard like my mates in school, I too could have become a doctor or engineer."

He was apprehensive about the upcoming reunion and what they might think of him. But when he sat in his Benz car chauffeured by a white driver, his doubts vanished.

"Not bad, not bad at all," he thought with a smile.

Looking at his driver, he recalled with dry irony the speeches of Powell lamenting about how brown people had stolen their jobs away!

With the growing numbers of South Asians in these cities and towns, the native whites gradually moved out, as they felt foreign in their own birthplaces. Indians had transformed them into "little Indias" that no longer looked or felt like the places they grew up. An irony of ironies.

Temples and mosques came up side by side, just as in Hyderabad! For the most part, the two communities got along well, as if united against a common enemy. As in the

1857 war of independence that Mr Husain, the history teacher, had taught them, the answers to the questions he posed about Hindu-Muslim unity still eluded him. Perhaps it depended on where the question was asked. The violence in India sometimes spilled over to Birmingham, reminding him that old wounds can open quite unexpectedly.

The Patels had Muslim friends as well. Their relationship was cordial and functional. They were looking forward to the reunion. In a few months they would be with his friends of fifty some years. He pulled out his old album and found a few black and white pictures from way back. He concentrated on the Golconda photo. It was such a long time ago. The characters seemed to haze as the rays of sunlight falling through the skylight of the ceiling burned through them.

He looked out of the window. It was a spring afternoon in Birmingham. The sky was blue, the sun warm, and the grass green, with hyacinths, lilacs, and tulips competing with each other for prominence in his back garden.

CHAPTER 13
Unbound and Free

Memory is an unreliable companion
As it remembers per its discretion

Vancouver, B.C. February 2019

Prabu and Mohini arrived in Edmonton, a western province of Canada, some fifty years ago. When he graduated from medical school in the early seventies in Hyderabad, there was jubilation in the housing complex. He was the first person from the "backward class," a label and identity that would be identified with his name forever, to become a doctor. A cherished dream was now a reality. Even though he had qualified for admission to medical school through the "reservation class quota," as it was called, he graduated with flying colours, topping the class in medicine. Prabu felt vindicated and determined to prove his worth as a physician.

His father distributed sweets to everyone in the office. His boss congratulated him and said that he may no longer need to work as a peon. His stock and status catapulted. Becoming a doctor was like winning a lottery that improved his fortunes. The neighbours in his community came over to congratulate him. One of them brought a garland of roses to place around his son's neck.

Prabu got his first job as a medical officer in the infectious diseases hospital in town. This was a government job that came with the likelihood of frequent transfers. As he was an eligible bachelor with a medical degree, offers started pouring in from his community. Like often married Like.

Marriages took place within one's caste with few exceptions. The dowry system was just as prevalent in the lower castes. The Gintys settled on Mohini. Her father worked at the train station as a booking clerk. A dowry of five thousand rupees was fixed. She had just finished high school and was taking typing and shorthand lessons with the intention of applying for a secretarial job at the same school where Mr. Ginty worked. Prabu met her at a wedding and liked her simplicity and dignity. The two fathers thought they would make a good match and their wives concurred. The marriage was arranged.

The wedding was a simple affair with little fanfare. A cleric from a family of *dalit* priests officiated the ceremony. Wearing a sacred thread around his bare shoulders, with sandalwood paste smeared on his forehead and arms, he looked every bit like a Brahmin priest in a cream coloured *dhoti*. The invitations went out with "cash gifts only" specified at the bottom of the card. About a hundred people, mostly from the housing complex, attended. The principal of the school where Ginty worked graced the occasion. A simple meal was served. At the reception, ice cream and cool drinks were offered. Prabu's friends Ramu, Vas, and

Rashid attended the ceremony. The others had already left the country.

Mohini moved in with her new husband's family on the first day of marriage. The Gintys partitioned the family room with a makeshift curtain and fashioned a bedroom for the newly married couple. Mohini gradually settled into her role as "daughter-in-law." She helped Mrs. Ginty in the kitchen, did chores, like hanging the clothes on the rope line to dry, ironed them, and swept the floors. She took a shine to Prabu's sister, Swarna, and found an ally in her. She was of her age and understood what it might be like to be shoved into a family of strangers.

In addition to the chores at home, she worked part-time in Mr. Ginty's office. Father-in-law and daughter-in-law walked back home together from work at the end of the day. Mohini usually kept a few paces behind as a mark of reverence. Prabu did his best to help his young wife adjust in her new role. He took her to the movies on weekends. She enjoyed this outing very much and looked forward to it.

This was the only time they could be together. They chatted about work, home, and their future. Prabu told her that he was looking for jobs in Canada. He heard that there was a shortage of doctors there, and they were recruiting graduates from other countries. Doctors from India had a leg up as they were educated in English and could communicate with patients. It was also not difficult to obtain a visa. He skimmed the Canadian medical journals in the hospital library for openings.

An ad from the Alberta Health Services caught his attention. They were looking for young medical graduates and were offering attractive salaries of 75,000 dollars a year. The deal was sweetened with free housing and a tax-free incentive grant of 5,000 dollars a year for two years. Permanent residency was assured at the end of the first year. No job offer in India came close to this. He read that the summers were hot and winters very cold. Plenty of snow was promised in the winter months. But he had no idea what that meant, as he had never seen snow in his life!

He decided to apply.

A month went by, and then a registered envelope arrived with his name and address printed on it. The Queen's stamp mark lent an aura of importance. Prabu palpated the thickness before opening it gingerly. This contained documents that would change his life. It was an offer of appointment for a year with extension to a second subject to satisfactory performance. There were details of how to apply for a visa and medical license to practise in this "energy province" of Canada. Necessary forms with the address of the Canadian high commission in Delhi were enclosed. There was a checklist of documents required to confirm his date of birth, medical degree, transcripts of marks, a valid passport, and a current photograph. He also needed a marriage certificate to confirm that Mohini was his spouse. A bank draft of thousand rupees was required as a processing fee. The process felt like an inquisition. To have to confirm that he was who he was and not an imposter. He was overwhelmed by the deluge of documents and did not know where to begin.

Over the years, his father, Mr. Ginty had helped professionals from various disciplines to get access to the principal. They sought favours for their sons and daughters. Admission to good schools with instructions in English were in high demand. In return for his help, they promised to return his favour whenever he needed their help. He maintained a list of their names and phone numbers just in case. The time to seek their help had come. He had accumulated enough "goodwill" to call it in.

He reached out to them and procured the various government documents needed for his son's visa. He obtained the marriage certificate from the "Registration and Stamps Department" and had the principal endorse it as a witness to the wedding. All the documents were notarized for authenticity. He put them all in a manila envelope from the principal's school supplies and personally mailed his son's application to the Canadian visa office. It was sent by registered post as required. He kept a photocopy of the documents in his safe custody. Mr. Ginty was delighted with his accomplishment, as he had pulled off a task that would ordinarily take months. His years as a lowly peon mattered when it counted!

Within a month of mailing the documents, Prabu received a temporary work permit and a temporary medical license to practise for a year. He was thrilled that his hard-earned medical diploma was recognized by a foreign country!

Mohini also received a visa as his spouse. Prabu was excited but with a sense of trepidation. He had never left home or flown in an aeroplane before. The thought of leaving his parents behind to fend for themselves weighed heavily on him. They had given him their all. Sacrificed everything for him. His guilt was assuaged by the excitement of beginning his life journey with Mohini in a far-off country. He was leaving one nest to build another.

The Gintys were excited for him. They were proud that their son was "foreign bound," an honour conferred only on a lucky few back then. They left India in the month of December of 1974 to start his new job on the first of January of 1975 in a foreign land that few had heard of. It was not America or England that everyone had heard and dreamed of, but Canada.

The Gintys saw them off with tears of joy. They were confident that the "foreign country" would bring professional success and prosperity to their son. They prayed for his health and welfare. They expected nothing at all in return. They were grateful that he had broken out of the "backward class" mould. Nothing could hold him back now.

The unsuspecting and naive couple arrived in Edmonton, Canada in the thick of winter. The documents that Mr. Ginty had laboriously obtained were verified and accepted. The immigration official welcomed the shy couple with the salutation, "Welcome to Canada," words that were music to their ears. They would be carved in their memory forever.

A snowy blizzard with an outside temperature of minus twenty degrees centigrade awaited them. It was like stepping out on a planet in outer space. The winter coats they had bought in India were hopelessly inadequate to combat the icy chill. Their hands and feet began to clamp, and their earlobes were numb. The five minutes it took for a taxi to arrive seemed like an eternity!

As the taxi drove them to their hotel, they looked out of the window. They saw majestic snow-covered mountains, rolling plains, and beautiful blue lakes for the first time. It was a sharp contrast to the flat brown landscape of Hyderabad. The buildings were covered with heaps of snow, and the trees were barely visible under the white canopy. They saw pedestrians walking on sidewalks bundled up in layers with their faces masked by woolen balaclavas. Their hands were wrapped in gloves and feet covered with boots up to their knees. They had never seen anything like this before.

Finally, they reached home. It was close to the hospital. The driver helped them with their suitcases and warned them to step out carefully.

"Watch out for black ice," he said.

Mohini was confused as everything she saw appeared white in colour!

Prabu and Mohini adjusted to a new country and learned new ways. They interacted with the locals and integrated with their compatriots. The hospital became the hub for making new acquaintances. There were a few Indian doctors who had arrived before them. Their son, Avi, was born a year later. He was born a Canadian citizen. They became Canadians two years later. Prabu referred to the new passport as his most prized possession. It was the smallest but the most important book he owned.

He trained as a psychiatrist and worked in Edmonton for ten years. He was posted as a staff psychiatrist in a mental hospital. This was a new experience for him. The atmosphere on the inpatient units was unpredictable. It swung from relative calm to commotion within minutes. Everyday brought new challenges. The patients seemed severely disabled. He learned that recovery was slow, and cures were rare. It was gratifying when he could even make a small difference to them and their families.

Mohini found a job in the bank as a teller. They bought a modest two-bedroom with a huge front and back yard. It was great value. They owned a lot of real estate for half the price one would have paid in cities like Toronto, Montreal, or Vancouver. They owned two cars and had a two-car garage. Prabu made monthly deposits of a hundred dollars to his father.

That was a fortune in rupees. The Gintys retired and moved to an independent flat in jubilee hills, thanks to his son's generosity. His sister, Swarna, got married to an engineer. Prabu and Mohini made a trip to Hyderabad to attend the wedding. The family had at last moved out of the run-down housing project that had been their home and community for so many years. They were born and bred there. That was the only world they knew. They now found themselves in new communities that they were not accustomed to. They were not sure how they would be received. This was a problem they did not have before.

Prabu visited Vas, who had settled in Hyderabad with his wife, Savitri, and their two children. He visited Rashid, who was married and had three children. He inquired about his parents and learned that they still resided in the old city. Prabu requested him to remember him to his parents. He cherished the memory of his visits and often recalled his mother's hospitality. How she had served him a meal in the family chinaware. They promised to keep in touch. No one knew where the rest of the gang was. It seemed like they had all vanished.

Prabu visited his parents regularly. The country seemed to be in transition in the nineties. The one-party congress rule had given way to coalitions of convenience. The liberalization policy brought new prosperity to the middle classes. With it came competition and unbridled capitalism. The BJP, a Hindu party, defeated the congress in the national elections. Tensions flamed with Pakistan. A new narrative began to take hold of public imagination. History was being revised. The new narrative said that Gandhi and Nehru had sold them out by kowtowing to the minorities. Fault lines began to reappear between Hindus and Muslims. Hindus and Muslims turned to religion and faith for strength and identity. The country was splitting into two, with each half staking its claim for pre-eminence.

Prabu felt that the Hyderabad he knew no longer existed. It was different from the past, which was not perfect, but had been relatively peaceful.

He wondered about Rashid, how he might be, and where his parents were. He asked Vas to track him down. This was in passing, the sort of conversation one has without any expectation.

Avi, their son, did well in school, ranking consistently among the top three students of the class. After high school he attended college in Edmonton and then gained admission to the engineering school in the university of British Columbia. It was in that year that The Gintys visited them in Canada. Prabu bought their air tickets for their first ever trip to a foreign country. In fact, they had not even seen many places outside Hyderabad in India.

Mr. Ginty marvelled at the clean streets and orderly traffic in Canada. He couldn't believe that no one honked on the road and yet travelled at such high speeds. They loved seeing their grandson and were proud that he would become an engineer some day. They hoped to be alive to see it. Prabu drove them all the way from Edmonton to Vancouver to show them the Rockies. It was an out of body experience for them.

The Gintys were awestruck. "This feels like heaven," they said. They promised to return for their grandson's wedding.

Mr. Ginty returned home a very happy man. He mused about that day years ago when he mailed the documents of his son. It had paid off. He took many pictures of his visit and showed the album to anyone he met.

Prabu was in his sixties when they moved to Vancouver. Avi was already in school there. He figured that Vancouver may be a better place to retire. He traded snow for rain and decided to move. They would also be closer to their son who was attending university. He negotiated a contract with the Vancouver mental health services for a position as chief of psychiatry. Mohini was able to get a bank transfer to a CIBC branch in Vancouver. They said their goodbyes to Edmonton and their friends. Edmonton had been their first home in Canada and would always hold a special place in their heart.

They discovered Vancouver to be a beautiful bustling city, nestled by the sea and mountains. Its beautiful swath of land shared the border with the USA. They blended easily into the mix of different cultures and ethnicities. As a province, it led the way in diversity, and they loved the way it came alive with outdoor activities in spring. Prabu liked to quote the New York Times excerpt, "You're gorgeous, you're sophisticated, you live well . . . Vancouver is Manhattan with mountains. It's a liquid city, a tomorrow city, equal parts India, China, England, France, and the Pacific Northwest. It's the cool North American sibling."

He referred to life as his "Canadian Dream."

Their son Avi met Reena in Seattle. Her parents had moved from Bombay in the seventies. Her father worked in Boeing. The wedding took place in Seattle. Prabu tried to get his parents over but they were now in their eighties in a retirement home in Hyderabad. A long flight was too daunting. They were delighted when their first great-grandson arrived a year later.

Their daughter, Ramani, who lived in Hyderabad, gave them a granddaughter. They added the baby pictures to the album. Ramani kept a close eye on them in the retirement home and spoke regularly to her brother in Canada to keep him informed. She was also caring for her in-laws who were living with them.

Their son, Avi urged them to move to Seattle. Prabu and Mohini declined, as they were nervous about the healthcare system in the USA. Besides, they were alarmed by the wave of nationalism and anti-immigrant sentiment sweeping the country. They preferred to retire in Canada. Prabu was a lifelong liberal and felt a loyalty to the party and the Trudeau family. But for his famous father he would never have emigrated.

Mr. Ginty became ill and passed away at the age of eighty-five. Prabu returned home to perform his duties as the only son. He invited his mother to come and live with him. She was hesitant and preferred to remain in the home. She had made friends there and the services offered were good, but she was overcome with grief. She died a year later of a broken heart. She and her husband had been soul mates.

They lived "A selfless life of service," as Prabu remembered with gratitude. They did so much for so many for so long without ever expecting anything in return. "Consistent with the teachings of *Gita*," Prabu told his son. "Action is thy motto. Fruit is not thy concern."

He may have been born as a person from the "backward class," but to all who knew him he was a prince among men.

Prabu retired at seventy with a decent pension, happy marriage, house fully paid up, son married and well settled, and a sister in India still close to him. He felt a contented man until the heart attack hit him like a bolt from the blue. The memory of that fateful day was vivid. He was woken up by a heaviness in the chest. It grew heavier into a stabbing pain, as if a rock inside him was threatening to burst out.

"Maybe something I ate," he thought. He sipped water from the glass next to him and closed his eyes, hoping it would go away. But it was stubborn and knocked on his chest again. And then again. Tiny drops of moisture began to form on his brow. He couldn't breathe normally. Now he could no longer pretend. Being a doctor, he knew what it was. The writing was on the wall. He initially hesitated to wake Mohini. He didn't want to frighten her. But the pain was unforgiving. Another crushing squeeze followed. This took his breath away.

Now he was petrified and nudged Mohini. She woke up with a start.

"What is it?"

"I think I am having a heart attack. Call 911," he said.

She dialled the numbers nervously and told the voice on the other end what she had just heard. "Shall I call Avi?"

"No, it's too early. Let's not alarm him."

She then remembered one of the ladies mention in a party recently that aspirin helps before the ambulance arrives. She ran to the kitchen and rummaged through the medicine cabinet frantically. She found the bottle and inverted a few tablets into the palm of her hand. She crushed these on the counter with a pair of tongs, swiped the powder into a glass of orange juice, and gave it a swirl. Then she rushed it to Prabu. He drank it like a magic potion.

The ambulance arrived soon with sirens blazing. They were loud and decisive. Now it was public. The neighbours would soon find out.

The paramedics soon appeared in their short sleeved green shirts and cargo pants. "How are you, sir?"

"A little tight here," he muttered, pointing to his chest.

"Relax, sir. We are going to move you over to a gurney, start a drip and hook you up to oxygen."

"Thank you. Where are you taking me?"

"To St Joe's."

Then the ambulance sped away with flashing warning lights on a highway that was desolate and empty. Once in the hospital, the hand-off was like a relay team. Smooth and swift. For Prabu, it was a blur. When he woke up, he was told he had the bypass surgery.

The idea of the reunion came to him while he was recuperating from the heart attack. A sense of mortality, perhaps nostalgia, maybe even some guilt, ignited a desire to reconnect with the gang. He thought it would be comforting. It was also time to close the circle. And to remind

themselves who they were, to understand who they are. That was when he started to track them down. One after the other.

And the conference call followed.

The heart attack had left its imprint. He looked dour with a furrowed brow. He coloured his hair black to camouflage the weariness of ageing. The dark shadows under his eyes denoted a life of struggle. He was emotional and broke down at the drop of a hat.

Mohini aged with him, losing her usual calm and serenity. She had come close to losing him. Her face looked grim and walked with a slight hunch, as if worn down by the weight of his illness. She went to the temple regularly for prayer and solace. At home, she prayed to *Lord Venkateshwara*, the family deity in the sanctum space in the pantry. She plucked a rose or a red hibiscus from her garden every morning and placed it at the Lord's feet. After lighting the lamp, she prayed for her husband's health. Prabu, too, joined to offer his own thanks for saving him from death's door.

Life was now in transition. It was time to lighten the load. Both materially and philosophically. Like the feline philosophy of living by unburdening. They were looking for a condo to downsize as they were finding it difficult to manage the house. It was an appropriate time to reappraise priorities. They worried about their son due to the political changes in the USA. Hate crimes and shootings were on the rise. They encouraged their son to move back to Canada, but he reassured them that Seattle was safe as they lived in Richmond, which was a safe Indian enclave.

The countdown to the reunion began. Another month to go. He was getting excited. His rehab brought him new confidence. He passed the stress test and the doctor waved the green flag to fly.

His thoughts began to wander back. He wondered if they would all be on the same page. Would their recollections coincide?

The history lesson, the questions Mr. Husain posed, the Golconda trip, the combined studies and walks on tank bund. All these images played before him like a reel from an old film.

CHAPTER 14

The Native Son

A travel back into the known
Is a plunge into the unknown!

Hyderabad, India February 2019

Vas was the only one in the gang of six to remain in Hyderabad, India. He and Savitri made their home in Anand Nagar, a middle-class housing colony in Hyderabad. In fact, this was the family home his parents built that they inherited. His brother, Rishi, had settled in America and ceded his claim to his brother. It had a small yard in the back and in the front. The gate opened out to a street that had transformed from a quiet road to a buzzling thoroughfare. The traffic was unyielding day and night, only taking a nap between midnight and five o'clock in the morning.

What used to be a safe neighborhood during his parents' days now experienced regular break-ins. People padlocked their front and back doors from inside, only letting people in after checking who they were by having them announce their names loudly after they knocked, like a prison guard letting visitors in after checking their ID. The housing society hired a retired army *jawan* as watchman to make rounds in the night. He carried a baton that he knocked against an electric pole or gate randomly to reassure residents that he was "on duty" and watching over their property.

The blue front gate looked battered and bruised and opened just wide enough to allow their Maruti car to be driven in or out by their driver Zafar, who was employed part-time. Zafar lived in the old city and was summoned whenever they needed to go shopping, visit their son, or attend a wedding. He had been with them for the last five years. He had four children, all under the age of ten. Whenever he spoke about them, he invoked *Allah's Grace* by pointing his hands upwards in humility.

He was paid a fixed amount of five thousand rupees a month in addition to tips when he was called upon to drive after working hours. He had a similar arrangement with another family, making a monthly wage of ten thousand rupees a month. He straddled the two jobs seamlessly.

Vas booked him by calling him on his mobile phone. Every driver in town owned one. They had to plan at least three days in advance. He rode his moped to work and back. This was the only way he could keep time. Taking public transportation meant having to take two buses plus a fifteen-minute walk. Savitri served him lunch or dinner, depending on the time of his assignment. They trusted him implicitly. This was a reputation he had gained over time.

The Sharma family home had fallen into partial ruin. The paint work was peeling, and cracks coursed through the walls like snakes. Like its occupants, it showed the effects of ageing. But memories had been made and stored in it.

These were intact and indestructible. Both the ancestral home and the Sharmas seemed resilient with their dignity intact despite the ravages of time. Savitri injected new life into an old house by planting beautiful plants in the front and back yards bearing white, blue, and pink flowers of various shapes and sizes.

Sunflowers, marigolds, daisies, and roses in different hues added character. The bougainvillaea in the front gave their home an earthen charm, hobbling over the gate and the compound wall in white, red, and pink tones. She often remarked that it thrived despite her benign neglect!

The vegetable patch produced a rich harvest of tomatoes, chillies, and brinjals that she shared with her neighbours. She loved sniffing the aroma of the mint and curry leaves that she used to spice and garnish her cooking.

Vas and Savitri aged gracefully. They had maintained their values despite a world that changed constantly around them. Their lives seemed to be well examined and well lived.

Vas's journey had been conventional. After graduating from high school, he went to the engineering college in Hyderabad and earned his electrical engineering degree. He found a job in the public works department as an entry-level engineer. His responsibilities included testing and maintaining motors and power generators, communication systems of the city, and writing detailed reports of his various assignments.

Two years into his job, his parents arranged his marriage with Savitri, the daughter of a colleague of Mr. Sharma's. She had earned a diploma in home science from the women's college. She became a social worker in the public health department, advising women about nutrition and family planning. Their marriage was a simple affair in a wedding hall that accommodated about three hundred people. The invitees were mostly neighbours, relatives, and office colleagues. Both Rashid and Prabu attended with their wives. They were newly married as well.

Vas and Savitri lived in a joint family set up. Their parents gave them their privacy. Father and son got along well. So did the mother and daughter-in-law. Mrs. Sharma ran the kitchen, instructing his wife Savitri about the idiosyncrasies of her son and husband in regards to their tastes and preferences. Their daughter, Savita, and son, Arun, arrived in quick succession. The grandparents and grandchildren adored each other. They seemed to have a special connection. Grandpa and Grandma passed on information about family traditions and gave them the real scoop on family stories that they would not hear from anyone. Seeing his parents spend time with his son and daughter reminded Vas of his special bond with his own grandfather.

He was promoted to the supervisor position after five years of service. Their children walked to the Catholic schools close by like the one he and his friends had attended. He rode his lambretta to work, dropping his wife first and picking her up on his way back home. The senior Sharma collected his grandchildren after school every day and Mrs. Sharma attended to them until their parents got home.

The nineties and beyond brought great change to Hyderabad. Globalization and liberalization brought software and IT industries to the city. A new hi-tech city was born outside the old one. It was christened "Cyberabad." It connected its call centres to cities around the globe through the magic of cyber technology. Smartly dressed young men and women with ID tags learned to speak in foreign accents. They served customers of companies in North America and Europe.

Rural villages and towns around Hyderabad were also beginning to urbanise. Flyovers and ring roads were built to ease traffic jams. New cinema halls and fancy restaurants sprung up all over the city. They were swanky and posh. People went to ritzy malls to do their shopping. Mosques and temples grew in numbers, each trying to outnumber the other. Political changes gave rise to communal tensions especially in marginalized lower caste and class Hindu and Muslim communities. In the midst of these changes, Bollywood surpassed Hollywood in terms of the number of movies they produced and the worldwide audience they commanded. Aamir Khan, Salman Khan, and Shah Rukh Khan, the three handsome Bollywood Muslim actors, stole the limelight by dancing and romping into the hearts of moviegoers. They did so without even having to change their muslim names, unlike Mohammed Yusuf Khan, who, back in the day, morphed into the famous "Dilip Kumar."

The old city became a flashpoint of violence. Vas kept in touch periodically with Rashid until they did not anymore. Politicians on both sides of the divide fanned the flames of hatred. It seemed like the old British ethos of "divide and rule" had been reignited. Frictions grew into squabbles that mutated over time to bitter conflicts and riots. This rippled to other cities and states as well. People turned to religion for peace and solace. Fissures developed in the composite culture of a city that had held it together for centuries.

Vas retired as a senior engineer with a good government pension and superannuation. Their savings had grown into a sizable sum, thanks to the high interest earning safety deposit account that he contributed to regularly. Vas and Savitri considered themselves luckier than the millions in the country who lived on the fringes of poverty.

"I am happy with my station in life," Vas often asserted.

His parents lived into their eighties before succumbing to old age. After his mother died, his father lived with him for a few more years. He was glad that his children experienced what he had in his childhood: the doting attention of grandparents who were indulgent to them and gave them of their love most abundantly and extravagantly. What a priceless gift!

Vas aged into a tall and lanky man with a wrinkled face, sunken eyes, and a sunburnt complexion. He stood straight as a rod. Mr. Serious felt better than he looked. Savitri had blossomed into a radiant, grey-haired woman with a winning smile that exuded confidence. They both seemed to enjoy good health, except for some arthritis and cataracts. Vas bragged that his vision was twenty/twenty after the eye surgery and the new lens implants.

Their son Arun, now a doctor, kept an eye on them and took care of their minor medical concerns. He visited them regularly. He and his wife often left their six-year-old son with them, sometimes for a sleepover as well. They spoiled him thoroughly and called him their "bundle of joy." Their daughter, Savita, was married to a software engineer in

The Reunion

Bangalore and had a five-year-old daughter whom they adored. Vas and Savitri loved their visits to Hyderabad when they came in December to escape the cold spell of Bangalore. They were delighted to have both their son and daughter together under the same family roof. They were back to the "original four," as Vas would often comment.

They were especially fond of their daughter-in-law, who was kind and caring, often bringing food, sweets and other goodies she had made. Savitri made it a point to pack something special she had made for her son in return.

Vas enjoyed his daily walks with Savitri at sundown. He loved reading novels that he borrowed from the library, and met his office colleagues for coffee at the Anand Bhavan cafe to discuss politics. Discussions of late were becoming heated due to differing views on politics. He lamented that Hindu-Muslim relations was at a "low ebb" and that he had lost touch with Rashid. They were both to blame. He heard that he had returned from *Hajj* with a beard and skull cap. He was equally intrigued by his Hindu friends who painted their faces with religious symbols. The clashes during festivals made him sad. He liked the economic policies of Modi of lifting the plight of poor people and infusing a new sense of national energy and pride. He also admired the fact that he had risen from humble beginnings. But he did not agree with the divisive politics. This had reopened old fault lines.

His colleagues often disagreed with him, stating, "We are a Hindu nation just as Pakistan is a Muslim nation and the USA is a Christian nation."

The arguments led to tensions within the group until they decided to avoid politics and religion in their discussions to keep the peace. Vas noticed that his friends had also become more religious and made it a point to go on pilgrimages to see old temples in far off corners of the country. This was new. This fervour was more recent. He felt detached from the new doctrine of politics. Arguing against it was like swimming against the tide. A sense of anomie described his isolation well.

Now, in the second decade of the 2000s, the changes of the nineties seemed to have hardened. Hyderabad seemed to be teeming with different identities based on caste, class, and religion. Although there were egalitarian forces trying to unite them, the prevailing current seemed headed in the opposite direction.

Vas began to prepare for the reunion. The conference call created excitement that stirred up old feelings. It rekindled a flame that had been on pilot for decades. The travel agent requested a multitude of documents including tax returns, property statements, and a police clearance certificate. He received a sponsorship letter from Vir to support his visa application to the USA, and a letter from Ramu for the Canadian visa. He received the visas and made travel plans.

He planned to visit Ramu in Toronto for a week and Ramu would drive him and Prabu to Vir's place in Michigan. He hoped that the reunion would reignite the old spark of friendship. Savitri attended to the electricity, water, and telephone bills as they could be cut off while they were away if they missed a payment. She also arranged with her neighbours, the Khans, to collect their mail and pop in once in a few days to make sure everything was okay. She paid the night watchman a hundred rupees to provide "extra patrolling" of their property. Her son promised to drive by their house on his way to and back from his clinic. He would go in periodically to give the impression that the house was occupied and not empty.

Vas made five prints of the old black and white picture of the gang at Golconda Fort as a momento. He had treasured it safely in his album. He hoped this would act as the ringer to arouse the alarm clock of memory. They had lain dormant for years. Savitri had the pictures framed as she heard that it was very expensive to do abroad. Vas felt that despite the access to social media, it was important to make a physical connection in real life.

He felt nostalgic about their time together in high school and considered it the best time of his life. They were "Footloose and fancy free," as he always described it. He recalled chatting with them for hours on end, swearing at each other, but with good humour, and not bearing any rancour or ill will. It was important to see if the relationship had endured and if they could reconnect like old times.

He was curious to find out. Seeing Facebook pictures or exchanging messages on WhatsApp was not the same as seeing them in the flesh to answer these questions. The conference call was just the opening salvo. The reunion would be the real thing. It would reframe old memories in the context of the present. Had their friendships withstood the impact of time, distance, and personal events?

An uneasy feeling of sorts took hold of him as he made the final preparations in the week before boarding the Air India flight to London and then Toronto. Vas's watch, which kept Hyderabad time, would soon change its clock back by several hours upon touching Canadian soil. Symbolic, he thought, of the journey back in time on which they were about to embark to the carefree days of school.

Would it be like reading an old fairy tale or dusting off of an old leatherbound journal, not knowing what the pages would reveal ?

CHAPTER 15
The Reunion

Does common history lead to common destiny?
Or do we write our own biography?

Michigan, U.S.A. July 4th Weekend

Prabu and Mohini arrived in Toronto from Vancouver on a warm June morning. After a five-hour red eye flight they were a little tired. They were looking forward to seeing Ramu and Padmini at the airport. This was Prabu's first flight after the heart attack. The doctor had warned him that sitting on a long flight was not good. He should walk up and down the aisle a few times and drink fluids. Dehydration and the confined space in the cabin could cause a clot to form. Mohini carried crushed aspirin powder in a small pouch just in case.

As soon as the plane landed, Mohini called Ramu, who was waiting in the free cell phone zone as they had discussed.

He said, "We will see you at the curb side in thirty minutes." He figured it would take that long to collect the baggage. As Prabu walked out of the terminal with Mohini wheeling the cart behind him, there was a slight wind which added a whiff of chill to the air. Each was looking for an older person who resembled the image they had of the other in their memory. And, sure enough, they locked eyes at first sight. They raised their hands simultaneously with a wave and smile.

The two embraced warmly as the wives looked on. It was as if the time gap of decades was bridged in a moment. The two women greeted each other with a half smile and a hug.

"Lovely to see you after all these years," said Ramu.

"Thank you. It is good to see you, too."

"You look good."

"Thanks, Ramu, I have had my problems recently," he said this with a hint of resignation and weariness in his manner.

Ramu relieved Mohini of the cart and loaded the suitcases into the trunk that popped open.

"How was the flight?" asked Padmini as the two ladies settled in the back seats of the Volvo.

"A long one. We boarded around midnight yesterday. Prabu couldn't get much sleep, he needs to rest up. "

"Yes, that will help," Padmini replied.

"This is a nice car," Prabu remarked.

"Yes, we are happy. I have had it for many years. We have only one car now."

There was a silence, and Ramu and Prabu looked pensive.

"I am really excited about the get together," Prabu said, breaking the pause.

"Me too. That's the CN tower." The needle looked hazy in the skyline due to the morning fog. "You should rest up today," Ramu added. He could see Prabu's wife Mohini nodding in agreement in the rear view mirror.

"Tomorrow we will give you a city tour," said Ramu.

"That's great. I haven't been in Toronto in years," replied Prabu.

"After Vas arrives, time permitting, we will take you to Niagara Falls," said Ramu.

"When is he getting in?" asked Prabu.

"Tomorrow morning, after a layover in London. He arrives on Canada Day."

"Any celebrations around here?"

"Yes, they will be launching some fireworks from the CN tower."

"Can we see it from where we are?" asked Prabu.

"Yes, we can. Hopefully it will be a clear day."

As he turned into the cul-de-sac, he added, "We will be home in a minute."

He pulled into the driveway. There were similar-looking homes on either side. It seemed a quiet and private street.

"How do you like living here?"

"It's a mixed bag. More privacy, but the last street to get plowed in winter."

"Prabu, you go inside. I will bring your luggage in," added Ramu.

"Thank you," Prabu responded, feeling a warmth in his friend's voice.

It was a well-lived home. The walls displayed family pictures and places they had visited over the years. There were souvenirs and artifacts from far off places. The leather couch looked worn with scuffs and scratches, with the colour fading on the cushion surfaces and arms. Prabu plopped himself into its sagging hollow.

Padmini had already laid the plates on the oval oak dining table. There was a stack of six brown wooden coasters engraved with *kalamkari* paintings from Hyderabad at the center of the oval. Embroidered white and red cotton napkins were neatly folded in halves and placed by the stainless steel half-size plates. She had cooked *upma* for breakfast with *chutney* and *sambar*. Prabu deposited their suitcases in one of the two guest bedrooms, the second waiting for Vas and Savitri.

"Prabu, why don't you relax for a bit and have a cup of coffee," said Ramu.

"That would be wonderful," replied Prabu.

The ladies made their way to the kitchen. "Hope Prabu is not too tired," Padmini remarked.

"I think he is. He should rest up for a while. He is also too excited to see Ramu," Mohini replied.

"Sorry about the heart attack. Must be hard on you."

"Yes, he has lost his confidence. Gets nervous easily," said Mohini.

"I can understand," sympathized Padmini.

"He thinks he is having a heart attack even when he feels a slight indigestion."

"Oh, really!"

"The doctor has prescribed Ativan to keep under the tongue when he panics," explained Mohini.

"Does it help?" asked Padmini.

"Yes, he takes it once every few days. Doesn't want to get hooked on it. He is also doing yoga these days."

The Reunion

The ladies seemed comfortable with each other talking about Prabu. Padmini was a good listener.

Ramu came down and sat next to Prabu, placing his arm around him. Drawing him closer, he whispered, "It's so good to see you after such a great long while."

"Me too." Prabu said, his eyes turning misty.

Then there was a silence. They didn't know what to say. They didn't have to.

Picking up the conversation a moment later, Ramu said, "We will drive to Michigan, spend a few days there and return on July fifth."

"I am so looking forward to it," said Prabu.

He then leaned back and surveyed the room. He tried to get a sense of Ramu through the pictures, the bookshelf, the artifacts, and the magazines on the coffee table.

"Are you fully retired?" Ramu inquired.

"Yes, Mohini insisted. We were looking forward to it. And then, bang! The heart attack. What about you?"

"Yes, I am retired. Enjoying every moment of it."

"Where are the kids?" asked Prabu.

"Rishi is in California. Stanford Law. Married Susan. Mina is in Chicago, married to a software engineer. Thank God, all are doing well. What about you?"

"My son Avi is in Seattle. Works for Microsoft. He married Reena. Nice girl. We are all fortunate and blessed."

"Yes, I agree," said Ramu.

"May I ask about your parents?" asked Prabu.

"Oh they are no more. What about your parents?"

"They too are deceased," replied Prabu.

153

They did so much for us. Remember your dad working as a peon? What a life of sacrifice," remarked Ramu.

Prabu was overwhelmed and began to sob. Ramu placed his hand on his shoulder, squeezing it gently.

Mohini walked in carrying a tray with two stainless steel cups of coffee. The foam at the top released the burnt aroma of fresh roast. Padmini followed and they both sat on the sofa across their husbands.

"We will call Vir later," Ramu said. "Let him know you have arrived."

"That will be nice. I haven't spoken to him in years. Looks like he has done very well for himself."

"Good for him," Ramu added. "He is quite wealthy, lives in a six-bedroom mansion in the country."

"Wonder what the Judge would have thought. A man of austerity," commented Prabu.

There was a pause. "Nice of him to host us," said Ramu.

"Yes, of course," Prabu chimed in.

As Ramu and Prabu enjoyed their breakfast in Toronto, Vas and Savitri were an hour into the Air India flight from Delhi bound for London. It was the first leg of a long flight. At Heathrow, they went through immigration and answered questions as to how long they would be in Britain. Vas answered they were there only for a few hours as transit passengers. The young officer spoke firmly and demanded to see their passports and travel documents.

Vas seemed absorbed in thought as the officer scrutinized the papers and wondered if Britishers had sought anyone's permission to occupy India for over two hundred years. Much longer, he thought, than a few hours in transit.

He doubted if the young officer had read history and was aware of British occupation in India. Highly unlikely, he suspected.. He doubted if he would know about the Indian war of Independence in 1857 and Freedom in 1947. Then he excused him for his brusqueness. Children are, after all, not responsible for the sins of their parents, he told himself. Or are they?

Ramu and Prabu were waiting for them in the arrivals lounge in Toronto. They had decided to come together to receive their friend. After answering more questions about the purpose of their visit, where and how long they were going to stay, and why they were having a reunion, they were allowed into Canada. Vas and Savitri felt as if they were subjected to a second inquisition in twenty-four hours. They came to expect it as an Indian passport was ranked low on the totem pole of passports. It was only in his album- higher than Pakistan or Afghanistan.

As they wheeled their luggage cart looking for Ramu, Prabu spotted a nervous-looking Vas. Savitri, dressed in a *saree*, was a few paces behind him.

"There they are," he shouted, waving a welcome.

Vas heaved a huge sigh of relief and started walking towards them.

The three friends huddled in an embrace. Ramu led the way to the parking lot, taking over the cart. The others followed.

"How are you?" Prabu asked.

"Fine, fine, a long flight."

"Any trouble with customs and immigration?" Ramu asked.

"Just the usual questions."

"They are usually more polite here than the Brits and Americans."

"Really? They all asked the same questions."

"Anyway, glad you are here," said Ramu.

"Yes, we are excited to meet everyone," agreed Vas.

"Padmini and Mohini are waiting to meet Savitri," said Prabu.

Savitri responded weakly, "Yes, I am also eager to see them."

As Ramu pulled his car away, Vas and Savitri looked out of the window as if they were watching a movie. They were impressed by the fast-moving cars keeping to their lanes and a double-decker truck trailer carrying a stack of brand new cars. He thought of the traffic in Hyderabad and vehicles driving bumper to bumper, honking intermittently, and weaving in and out willy-nilly. Not an inch of space was left for pedestrians.

These were two different worlds, he thought. Kipling's ballad, "East is East, and West is West, and never the twain shall meet," came as an epiphany.

They were home in an hour. Ramu and Padmini escorted them up and deposited their suitcases in the second bedroom. The three friends were reunited after five decades.

"How are things in Hyderabad?" asked Prabu.

"It's a different world than the sixties," said Vas.

"How so?" asked Ramu.

"Very crowded, software industries, a lot of prosperity."

"May I ask about your parents?" asked Ramu.

"Both of them are gone. I live in the same house."

The Reunion

"Did they live with you," asked Ramu.

"Yes, that was a great boon for the kids. My dad passed away just a few years ago."

"I am sorry to hear that. He was a good man," said Ramu.

"How is politics in Hyderabad?" asked Prabu.

"A tug of war between the Hindu and Muslim Parties. Modi and Owaisi are the two prophets," replied Vas.

"Any news about our school?" asked Ramu.

"Still there. You need to cough up a couple of lakhs of rupees to get your kid admitted," said Vas.

"That is expensive. Who can afford it?" enquired Prabu.

"The young techies can. They earn a lot and spend a lot," said Vas.

"Not like our days. We believed in saving for a rainy day."

"Not anymore. They know how to enjoy life."

"Any news about our teachers?" enquired Ramu.

"They are all dead except Mr. Hussain, I think," answered Vas.

"Have you seen him lately?" asked Ramu.

"Yes, once with Rashid and Kazmi. A few years ago," replied Vas.

"How were they?" Ramu and Prabu asked almost simultaneously.

"Mr. Hussain looked the same, but Rashid and Kazmi looked different. They had been to the Haj and were wearing traditional clothing, and had grown a beard."

The conversation ended.

"We will drive to Michigan on the weekend. Tomorrow is Canada Day. We can watch fireworks from a nearby park," Ramu said.

"How is it celebrated?" asked Vas.

"People generally party with friends, watch fireworks, have a beer. They watch the celebration in Ottawa on TV."

"What happens in Ottawa?"

"The Governor General hoists the flag and the Prime Minister addresses the nation. Fireworks and music. Various artists perform."

"How is the Quebec problem?" enquired Vas.

"Quiet right now," replied Ramu.

"I understand they want to separate from Canada?"

"Yes. There have been a few referendums on the issue of seperation."

"Sounds similar to the Hindu-Muslim divide in India," wondered Vas.

"What do you mean?" asked Prabu.

"The English French divide in Canada seems similar to the Hindu Muslim divide in India ," replied Vas.

"Yes, Canada is a country of two nations," agreed Prabu.

"As India is becoming a country of two nations," concurred Vas.

While the three friends were reconnecting in Toronto, Patel and Nalini were on the red eye to Detroit. Vir had promised to pick them up.

Patel visited all the jewelry store branches before leaving on his vacation. He settled outstanding bills and signed off on the payrolls. And arranged with his assistants to call him at seven o'clock in the morning, American time, to give a daily accounting of the sales and transactions. This reminded him of his uncle, Kantibhai, who sat down with the cashier at the end of the day for stock taking. He put

The Reunion

the daily account to bed and opened it the next day after a prayer.

Nalini arranged with her Indian neighbour to pop in daily, water her plants and collect the mail. She called the insurance company to inform them that they would be away and that someone would be entering their house daily to make sure the house was cared for in their absence.

Meanwhile, the stage was being set for the six friends to converge in Michigan. From three different continents, they would come together to find out if they shared a common life story. They were expectant, excited, and a little apprehensive. Would they recognize each other, laugh at the same jokes, and remember their teachers?

All would be revealed soon. It was like resuming a movie after an intermission of decades. To see the second half!

Many questions loomed on the horizon. Are memories a shared experience? Do friendships endure over time? Do we make our circumstances or are we made by them?

Roop and Madhuri arrived before the others by the Delta flight from Atlanta. He picked up the car rental at the Detroit airport and set the GPS for Vir's address. Vir and Meena were more than ready for their visitors. The weather in Michigan was in the eighties with humidity. The Srivastava garden was rich with chrysanthemums and geraniums in full bloom.

Squashes and pumpkins were in dirt abundance. Meena personally tended to the indoor begonias, succulents, and jades, and placed them in colourful pots. The automatic sprinkler system was on duty from dawn to dusk, watering the entire swath of their land. The gardener had cut the lawn with mathematical precision and trimmed the hedges perfectly by hand.

The housekeeper was summoned a week earlier to clean the house. The six bedrooms were prepared with beds made, sheets changed, and vases filled with fresh cut flowers from the garden. A heap of towels of various sizes were placed on the dressing table. They assigned the bedrooms randomly, except for the larger one which was reserved for Prabu and Mohini in view of his recent heart attack. All the six bedrooms were, therefore, spoken for. It was like a well-run hotel that had seen visitors come and go.

Meena made a quick tour of the premises like a housekeeping manager for a final check to dot the i's and cross the t's. Vir usually left these details to Meena, as he was confident that nothing ever slipped her attention. She was skilled in the "host role" and embodied it with aplomb.

He rearranged his plaques and accolades collected over the years to make sure they were in clear view. He especially treasured the "Entrepreneur of the Year" brass plaque which he displayed prominently on the mantelpiece. Meena dusted off her silver plated "bridge trophy" and placed it at the other end of the mantelpiece.

They were ready to welcome their friends. It felt like standing on a reception line to greet guests as they arrived. Excited and enthusiastic, they eagerly looked forward to playing their respective roles. They had perfected it over the years. It came as second nature to them.

The last thing on Meena's list before the guests arrived was her appointment with her hairdresser. She preferred short hair and dyed it brown. She was conscious that this hairdo made her look attractive and brought out her vivacious personality.

The friends arrived as scheduled. They were received warmly and settled comfortably in the allocated bedrooms in the mansion. It was the evening of July the third. There was an air of formality. They were not fully at ease. It was like making a reacquaintance rather than a reconnection. After all, they were seeing each other after fifty some years. Perhaps that would change soon, and they would loosen up.

They gathered in the huge family room with each of them finding a cosy place to settle. The girls were like satellites orbiting Meena, who was the leading star. They followed her cues and treaded gingerly to avoid any missteps.

Meena could sense the awe in them of their huge home. It was well appointed. There were carefully chosen furnishings, strategically positioned sofas and table lamps, artistically laid Persian carpets, and randomly scattered throws for warmth. Artwork from foreign countries and coffee table books from far off lands. Hopefully they would trigger a conversation about their travels.

The illuminated glass curio cabinets displayed a wide array of collectibles and antiques from India and Europe. There were delicate porcelain figurines from Lladro, Royal Doulton from England, and cut glass from Murano.

Meena was taking a measure of the ladies and their tastes and interests. She suggested a visit to the mall, maybe a manicure and pedicure, and a visit to the country club to meet her lady friends. They nodded meekly in agreement.

Once they were settled, Vir asked what they would like to drink. Patel asked for a single malt, Roop had rum and coke, and Prabu and Ramu ordered wine. Vas asked for orange juice. Vir filled his own glass with a single malt. The ladies settled for a margherita, except Savitri, who preferred orange juice like her husband.

"So, Vir, how are things?" Vas inquired, initiating a conversation.

"Fine thank you." replied Vir.

"Are you fully retired?"

"Yes."

"Is time easy to kill?" enquired Ramu.

"Yes, I have a routine. As my father used to say, if you don't kill time, time will kill you."

"How is the Judge?" asked Vas.

"He has passed on," informed Vir.

"I am very sorry. If I had known I would have visited him earlier," said Vas.

"It's all right. Any news about Rashid?"

"Not sure. I understand he has become somewhat religious," said Vas.

"How do you mean?"

"Has grown a beard and wears a Saudi style thobe."

"But he was not like that, not even his family," said Vir

"Yes. Everyone is more religious these days," replied Vas.

"In what way?"

"Hindus as well. Doing daily *puja* at home, going to temples regularly, and visiting holy sites has become very popular."

"Like going to Mecca?"

"Perhaps."

"What about you?" asked Vir.

The Reunion

"Same as before. Savitri and I just pray at home."

Cutting in, Roop asked, "What's the reason for the change?"

"I think there is an Islamic and Hindutva wave in India," replied Vas.

"One reacting to the other?" observed Roop.

"It would seem so," speculated Vas.

"Who is reacting to whom?" asked Vir.

"Hard to say. It's a vicious circle," responded Vas.

"Why do you think that is?" asked Prabu.

"Religion has become the rallying point for both."

"Is there a fear that Muslims will outnumber us in a few decades?" asked Roop.

"Perhaps. But misplaced. Four out of five Indians will still be Hindus"

"I wouldn't rule it out," said Vir.

"There is no statistical basis for it," clarified Vir.

Continuing the conversation, he said,

"I heard there is a 'Hindus for Trump' group here."

"Yes, I am part of it," answered Vir.

"Me too," echoed Roop.

"What is the reason for this?" Ramu asked.

"There is much in common in the politics of the two countries," said Vir.

"Really! How is that?" exclaimed Ramu.

"Well, both countries have issues with migrants, Islamic threats, and cultural differences."

"Do you really believe that?" asked Prabu.

"Yes," replied Vir emphatically.

"What do you think is the solution?" asked Prabu.

"Maybe we, too, should build a wall at the Bangladesh border. Fight Islamic terrorism and protect Hindu culture," responded Vir.

"That sounds Trumpian. Can't we fight terrorism without antagonizing millions of moderate innocent muslims ?" challenged Ramu.

"Well, we need a complete reset in our thinking," insisted Vir

"But I hear your president lies, cheats on taxes, and hates all immigrants," interjected Patel.

"His character doesn't matter," Vir said. "He is a patriot. A successful businessman. Believes in low taxes to incentivize the economy."

"But I heard that his slogan 'Make America Great Again' really means 'Make America White Again,'" Ramu opined, entering the fray.

"No, that is fake news. Left wing propaganda. Don't believe what you read in the papers or see on TV," Roop reacted.

"Where do you get your news?" asked Ramu.

"We get it from Fox. Most objective and unbiased," Roop responded.

Ramu and Prabu exchanged glances, not sure what to say.

"Another round of drinks?" Vir asked.

All said, "Yes." As if they needed one!

Meena walked in with a platter of *samosas* and *pakodas*.

"Don't get him started on politics," she said, pointing at Vir. "He is obsessed with Modi and Trump."

Madhuri piped in, "Roop as well."

Patel joined in. "Boris is also a friend of Trump."

"Did you vote for him?" asked Ramu.

The Reunion

"No, I didn't. Brexit is bad for my business. They are also against immigrants."

"Is that bad?" asked Vir. "We have illegals crossing into our country by the busloads."

"Weren't we immigrants when we arrived?" questioned Patel.

"Yes, but we were invited by them."

"Invited? I thought we came because we were needed to serve in hospitals and factories, like labourers."

"No, we were doctors and engineers, not labourers."

"It's another kind of labour, isn't it? To hire them as they had a shortage. Like farm workers from Mexico in America," asked Patel.

"Wonder how our fathers would have reacted to the leaders in India and America," Prabu interjected gently.

"Judge Saheb would not have supported either of them," said Ramu.

Vir was silent.

"What about Mr. Gopalan, your dad?" asked Patel.

"I don't think he would have supported them either," replied Ramu.

"Why not?"

"I think principles were important to them. They were Gandhian in outlook," said Ramu.

Roop and Vir took another gulp of scotch, maintaining their silence.

"So how are things in Canada?" Vir asked, changing the topic.

"Oh, same old same old," said Prabu.

"Heard it's a socialist country."

"Depends on how you understand socialism," replied Prabu.

"How do you understand it?"

"Well, having social programs like welfare for the unemployed, free health care, subsidized housing for the poor does not make it a socialist country."

"Isn't that the same as communism?"

"No. It is democratic socialism. Helping the poor within a free market economy," clarified Ramu.

"What's the difference," argued Vir.

"One is a democracy, whereas communism is state controlled authoritarianism," chipped in Ramu.

"And Canada is what?"

"Capitalism like yours, but with a conscience," replied Ramu.

"But someone has to pay for your conscience!"

"Agreed. One has to pay for one's values," responded Ramu.

"So, Prabu, did you have to wait for your bypass?" Roop asked, changing the topic.

"No. Got it the same day I went in," he replied.

"But we hear about your long waiting lists," said Roop.

"Yes, for hip replacements, cataracts, and such," said Prabu.

"Is that good?"

"We follow the principle of greater good."

"What does that mean?" questioned Vir.

"Looking beyond oneself to benefit others."

"You know, I have treated many Canadians who cross the border to get an angiogram or MRI urgently," said Roop.

The Reunion

"And I have treated many of your poor, mentally ill patients for free," shot back Prabu.

The alcohol was beginning to loosen tongues.

"Patel, your country also has free health care for all?" continued Roop.

"Yes. It's called National Health Service."

"Does it work?"

"I think so. I am still here!"

"Who pays for it?"

"General taxation. Like the rest of Europe. Like your Medicare. How do you like Obamacare?" asked Patel.

"A total disaster," replied Roop.

"Why is that?"

"Government run. Very inefficient. Delayed payments. Loss of revenue. They think we doctors earn too much," said Roop.

"But I heard it helped twenty million people get health care. Principle of Greater good?" said Prabu.

"Yes, but at our cost!" shot back Roop.

Another pause ensued.

"Dinner is served," Madhuri announced.

They made a beeline to the dining table, which had been set for twelve. The waiters from the Indian restaurant were on duty. They served them while Meena directed them through the courses. Vir filled their glasses with vintage wine. It cut through the tension that hung over them from the earlier conversation. The ladies chatted about movies, hobbies, pets, and travel, while the men concentrated on the food.

After dinner, Vir asked, "Anyone for cognac?"

All nodded except for Vas. The ladies joined them. Meena, Madhuri, and Nalini went for the night cap. The other ladies declined. The men nursed the drink as if they were sipping nectar.

Prabu excused himself for the night, saying he was tired, and Mohini followed him.

"Rest up," said Vir. "Will see you down for breakfast tomorrow morning." He gave Prabu a hug as he got up to leave.

The others chatted for a while longer, avoiding anything controversial. It was like sailing to safe harbour after wading through choppy waters. They then returned to their bedrooms.

As Prabu prepared to turn in, Mohini asked, "So, how was the evening?"

"It was okay, I guess. Vir is a good host. But the glue is missing. People change, I suppose."

Mohini sensed a little disappointment in him.

Vir and Meena wrapped things up for the evening. She loaded the coffee machine with ground coffee beans and water in the right proportions and set the timer for seven o'clock the next morning. They both walked up the winding oak staircase to their bedroom and prepared for the night.

Meena asked "Did you have fun?"

"Yes, it was fun."

"I heard your dad's name being mentioned. What was that about?"

"Oh that! They thought he wouldn't have voted for Trump or Modi."

"Why wouldn't he have?"

"Because he always said character is important." And then he turned the night light off. He was out like a shot.

The gang woke up to the birdsong of robins in the backyard at the crack of dawn. It sounded like a laugh or chuckle interrupted by a sharp peek. It was like an alarm call.

Vir and Meena walked down the stairs together in their expensive silk robes, enjoying the soft and buttery feeling of the cloth. They heard Patel in animated conversation with his assistant in England discussing the price of gold and silver in the market. The familiar aroma of brew with the sound of bubbling water and coffee dripping down the carafe portended the start of a new day.

Vir and Meena were a perfect couple. They did everything together. They had even grown to look like each other, sometimes having the same thought at the same time. They were sympatico and in tune with each other, always on the same wavelength.

It was July fourth, America's Independence Day. Vir walked over to the front door, deactivated the security alarm code, and opened the door. It was a special day. He wanted to make sure that the flag was properly displayed. Being conscious of the flag etiquette, he made sure it was hung vertically from the flagpole with the union and stars portion to the left and the lower portion just above the floor, not touching it. He saw Rick across the street tending to his flag and waved a hello. Rick waved back.

Patel followed, sliding his hand down the handrail of the bannister in his white *kurta* and *pyjama* with Nalini behind him. He displayed the ease of one who was comfortable in his skin and unphased by affluence.

As they waited for coffee, Vir asked, "So how is business?" How is gold doing?"

"It is trading higher at about one thousand dollars an ounce."

"Do you have to adjust the price of jewelry accordingly?"

"Yes, we fix the price of the item according to the price on the date of delivery."

"So, a customer may hold off buying until the price is lower?"

"Yes, these are games that people play. So, we fix the price at a level that will only protect them up to a certain threshold," added Patel.

"What's your profit margin?" asked Vir.

"About fifteen to twenty percent," replied Patel.

"How is your son doing?"

"Harish is a doctor. Doing well. Nice girl, his wife."

"How are your parents?"

"My mom passed away. Dad is in a retirement home," replied Patel in a sad tone.

"Can't he live with his brothers in the joint family?" asked Roop.

"No. They have all split up," replied Patel.

"Oh, I am sorry! Wouldn't your dad prefer to live with you in the UK?"

"No. He likes it there. Some of his friends are in the same home. They go back a long way."

"I can understand. My dad was also not interested," said Vir.

Vas, looking a little hesitant and shy, joined them with Savitri. She was clad in a *saree* with a beige *pashmina* shawl wrapped around her shoulders. All the others joined the circle.

"Hope everyone slept well?" Vir asked generally, not pointing to anyone in particular.

"Very comfortable," Vas replied.

"We replaced the mattresses recently," Meena added.

"Yes, very sturdy and firm," Ramu chimed.

"Let's all have coffee on the patio. We can sit on the deck," Meena said, opening the patio door.

"Excellent idea," Roop remarked and walked out to the deck.

Nalini made tea for herself and Patel.

They settled down in the chairs on the hardwood floor of the deck. As they sipped their coffee, they admired the intermingling redwood, pine, and cedar trees in the backyard with the grey rocks scattered randomly. It looked like a forest with the rays of the sun piercing through the canopy of trees.

"How is your brother, Rishi? I remember he left for Stanford," Vir said.

"He is in Silicon Valley. Very successful. Has two kids," replied Vas.

"Are you visiting him?"

"No just saw him in India when he came on vacation."

"Any news about our teachers?" inquired Vir.

"All gone," Vas replied. "The last one to go was Mr. Husain, our history teacher. He died of lung cancer. Was a smoker."

"I am sorry to hear that. He was always well prepared for the class."

"Yes. Do you remember his questions?"

"Not really. Had something to do with Hindu-Muslim unity I think," guessed Vir.

"That's correct," Prabu added. "About what happened between 1857 and 1947."

"Can you answer them now?" Roop asked.

"Too complex. Politicians on both sides have fueled animosity. Promoted fear and distrust of each other. Led to the deadlock in 1947 and the partition."

"Perhaps partition was the best thing. I can't imagine an India with another two hundred million Muslims," replied Vir.

"Why would you say that? Didn't we get along well back then?" asked Prabu.

"There would have been a permanent civil war. We would have had only two major parties. The Hindu and Muslim party. Imagine that!" said Roop.

"Some believe that as we have lived peacefully together for centuries, we could have done so again. Composite Nationalism where Hindus, Muslims, Christians, Sikhs, and Parsis share a common vision," chimed in Ramu.

"Dream on. That could never be a practical proposition. We would have split up into five different nations," said Vir vehemently.

"I agree." Roop said. "That would have been a disaster."

"We did not feel any rancour towards Rashid and Kazmi, and neither did they," Ramu reminded them.

"We were too young and naive at that time," said Roop.

"Or maybe we have developed those feelings later?" replied Vas.

The Reunion

And then changing the topic Vir inquired, "Any news of Mr. Jeevan?"

"He was fired before he died. Parents complained that he had interfered with young boys," Vas replied.

"Yes, he was a bastard. A pedophile," Ramu added, swallowing a lump in his throat.

The others looked perplexed. A hush hung in the air as if a bomb had just exploded.

Seizing the silence, Savitri produced the framed black and white pictures of the gang at Golconda Fort and went around handing one to each of the boys.

"Oh, this is so lovely. Brings back memories. I had forgotten all about that trip. Thank you so much," said Vir.

All the others were just as moved.

The ladies grabbed the pictures from their husbands and started looking at them. They were visibly amused at how young and naive their spouses looked.

As the conversation began to chafe, Meena sensed a need to avoid bellicose topics. Shifting the topic, she said, "So, tell us about your children and grandchildren."

This was a welcome segue. It occupied the next hour. They waxed in turn about their children's accomplishments and Ivy League education. The conversation flowed smoothly. They had obviously recounted and repeated these stories and anecdotes previously to others a million times. Soon the iPhones were out with pictures of the grands at various points of their chronological development. Exclamations of "Awesome," and "Wow," punctuated the colloquy. They bragged about the talented spouses they had married, adorable grandchildren they had produced, and daughters- and sons-in-law they had brought into the family. Then there was a stock-taking of parents, when they passed, who was left, and who was taking care of whom, and the siblings, and their whereabouts.

Meena emerged from the kitchen and corralled them for breakfast. They headed back to the dining table. The breakfast was a lavish spread with western and eastern dishes, vegetarian and non vegetarian offerings. They were spiced in varying degrees to satisfy every palate.

Meena reminded Vir to tell his friends about the dinner at the country club in the evening. She whispered in his ear to warn them of the dress code.

She then took them around the house on a guided tour. Every room was shown, and every nook and corner was revealed. Every bathroom, closet, and cupboard was opened and closed. She took them to the basement to show the gym, ping pong and pool table, and the fancy wine cellar and bar service. She salivated as she gleefully described the state-of-the-art mini theatre and projection room they had recently added. The guests were spellbound.

Vas asked if the house was too big for just the two of them and if they had considered downsizing.

Meena replied, "It's hard when you get used to the space. Besides, Vir likes to entertain a lot. The kids love coming here to watch movies."

At the end of the mini safari, the women folk retreated to their assigned bedrooms while the men walked around the house casually.

The Reunion

Meena and Madhuri sat together for a private tête-à-tête in the family room. "So how is Georgia. Do you like it there?" asked Meena.

"Yes, very much. It's been our home for years," replied Madhuri.

"But your kids are in New York and St Francisco?"

"Yes, unfortunately."

"Would you move closer to them?"

"No, we are going to retire in Georgia."

"We hear the crime rate is high in Marietta!"

"We live in the countryside. It is safe, with a good country club and a big Indian community in Atlanta. There is also a nice temple."

Their husbands, Vir and Roop, huddled to discuss politics. They were both campaigning for Trump's re-election for a second term.

Ramu, Prabu, and Vas lingered on the patio deck a while longer after the others had left.

"Looks like Vir and Roop have changed," Prabu remarked.

"In what respect?" asked Vas.

"You know, about our childhood, and so on. I thought we were kind of close with Rashid and Khazmi," Prabu remarked.

"I would say so," agreed Vas.

"I used to visit his house. His mom was very kind to me.. Always treated me well," recalled Prabu.

"I tried to reconnect with him a couple of years ago. He was busy with things. Said he was involved with helping the mosque raise money for teaching the Quran to the kids," added Vas.

"In Vancouver, the Hindu priest is offering lessons in Hinduism to the children," stated Prabu.

"You mean the children of the young parents who have migrated from India recently?"

"Yes."

"I don't remember insisting on our children to go to the temple or take lessons in Hinduism," Ramu chipped in.

"I agree, but young people in India today are more religious. They continue this when they come abroad," replied Prabu.

"Hmm! Thats interesting," said Ramu.

Patel and Nalini walked around in the backyard, enjoying the quiet and peace in the garden. They enjoyed walking on the pristine and soft lawn. It was a big change from the hurly burly of Birmingham.

Over the years, Patel had grown accustomed to his role as the "fifth wheel" of the gang. He was certainly not an outsider, but not quite as much of an insider either. This gave him the freedom to agree or disagree without offending anyone. When things got tense, he acted as the buffer that absorbed the shocks.

As the weekend wore on, the initial excitement began to wane. Memories and recollections had been jiggled. After lunch and a brief siesta, a visit to the temple was next on the itinerary. They had discussed and ruled out Niagara Falls. Ramu said he would take Prabu and Vas from Toronto. The travel agent had included it in the package for the Patels.

They headed out in two cars. Prabu sat in the van with Meena and the ladies. Vir drove the others in his Lexus which he had recently traded for the older model barely a couple of years after he had leased it.

The temple was an hour away in the suburbs. Vir explained to them that he was on the board and that they had purchased the land in an elevated area for privacy. Plenty of space for parking was a priority. He was one of the major donors.

The temple was an imposing white edifice in the midst of an ornate garden. It was manicured and had an impressive range of plants and flowers of various shapes and colours. The structure was geometrically symmetrical with figures of various deities carved into the stone. A spire on top of the cupola pointed to the sky. The central pond with floating lotus petals and jets of water falling from the fountains caught everyone's attention. Vir took a selfie picture of the group with the backdrop.

Meena led them straight to the donor wall in the large atrium entrance to the temple. Names of donors were Inscribed in descending order of amounts donated. On the top of the roll the words "THE SRIVASTAVA FAMILY: 100,000 Dollars," were engraved on the marble.

There were a few anonymous donors on the list.

Madhuri and Nalini congratulated her for their generosity. Inside the pillared hall were carvings, paintings, and deities that had been especially imported from India. With folded hands and a sense of ownership, Meena and Vir walked towards the divine core of the temple where the main idol of *Vishnu* was installed. Kids were running around playing games while their parents prostrated in front of the idols.

The head priest caught Vir's attention and approached him with "*Namasteji.*"

Vir reciprocated and introduced him to his friends. "Sharmaji has come all the way from Benaras. We are lucky to have him."

He performed a special service for the group. He lit a lamp, chanted some *slokas,* marked their forehead with *tilak*, and offered *prasad* on a silver plate consisting of fruit, nuts, and flowers. Meena thanked him profusely.

Vas fleetingly remembered the roadside *Ganesh* temple they had stopped by years ago on their way back from the Golconda trip before the exams. It seemed that their prayers had been answered. They were all successful in their journeys. Journeys that had however been different with different destinations.

Ramu, too, paused in front of the *Ganesh* idol in a pensive mood. He wondered if this is what they had prayed for. He was uncertain as to what success is and how to measure it. This was not easy to compute, he figured. Back then, he thought, they prayed for a new beginning. Now they were praying for a good ending.

On their way out, Vir directed them to the dining hall down the stairs by the entrance. He entertained them with light refreshments, a mini lunch of sorts, enough to sustain them until the grand July fourth dinner at the country club.

The drive back home was quiet. The reunion was gradually winding down. In a couple of days, they would return to their different ways of life. Vir told them he had invited a few of their Indian and American friends to meet them the next day.

The Reunion

Meena came down sharply at six after an afternoon nap. The temple visit had tired her. Now in her late sixties, she had developed some facial wrinkles and noticeable age spots. Due to a deficient thyroid she had gained about fifteen pounds in weight and her hair wasn't as thick as before. She insisted on keeping the temperature of the rooms up as she couldn't bear the cold. The Michigan winters were becoming a challenge to endure. Vir had similar issues with his arthritis. That is how the idea of a Florida resort was born. Their kids could also visit them there over the holidays.

Meena's penchant for dressing up for an occasion, however, had not slackened. For the special evening, she dressed youthfully in black pants and a full-sleeved, white, silk top, leopard striped shoes, a pearl necklace, and matching ear studs. A Gucci Bengal tiger pink scarf with a matching handbag completed the ensemble. Vir turned out in a black dinner blazer with dress pants and a crisp collared shirt and tie. Half an inch below his jacket sleeve displayed a pair of black-enamelled gold cufflinks. The Dunhill brand logo was conspicuously engraved on them. Both sides of the cuff were perfectly aligned. His black Oxford leather shoes looked shiny and glossy. He could easily use it's "mirror shine" to comb his hair if he placed his foot on a chair and bent slightly towards his reflection! He looked tall and frail with a dour demeanour but quite stately.

Roop was formally dressed with a dress coat and tuxedo while Madhuri appeared in an evening wear from Neiman Marcus that she had specially purchased for the event. The others appeared in a wide assortment of jackets, shirts, ties, pants, and shoes with gentle contempt for colour or coordination. The ladies wore their best pant suits or gowns, except for Padmini, who made a grand entrance in a blue *kanchipuram* silk *saree* with a brocaded gold border. The necklace she wore was her gold *mangalsutra* with the two medallions which represented the coat of arms of the two families. The necklace and *saree* were from the time of her marriage. She lit up the room.

"So, how long have you been a member?" Roop asked.

"About twenty years now. Initially I was declined, you know. Closed shop with membership for whites only. Kind of status symbol. Indians were not welcome," replied Vir.

"Why was that?" asked Vas.

"They thought we were not sophisticated enough to follow the etiquette."

"So how did you manage to get in?" inquired Vas.

"My white junior business partner sponsored me," said Vir.

"Sounds like applying for a visa!" quipped Vas.

"Similar, I suppose," replied Vir.

"Was there an interview?"

"Yes. They also made discreet inquiries about my standing in the business community."

"Are you a member of the Hyderabad or Secunderabad club in India?" Roop asked Vas.

"No, I never bothered. Besides, it is too hard to get in," said Vas.

"Really, why is that?"

"From the British days it has been exclusive. Membership is bequeathed from one generation to the next. Like family heirlooms."

"Can others apply?" asked Roop.

"Yes, there is corporate membership and a lottery once a year," said Vas.

"That's like a green card lottery!" said Roop with a chuckle.

"In a way, yes."

"You are not interested?" asked Roop.

"Not really. Quite elitist. Besides, it is hellish to drive through traffic from Hyderabad to the Secunderabad Club," replied Vas.

"Are there any other clubs?"

"Yes, many have sprung up. If you pay an initiation fee you can get in."

"How about you?"

"I am not interested. Can't afford it, either."

"Oh, I am sorry," exclaimed Roop.

"Don't be. I don't miss it. What do you get for the membership here?" Vas enquired.

"You can play tennis on beautiful acrylic hard courts, golf on a private course, socialize, dine. Whatever you please," interjected Vir.

"Do you play any sport?" asked Vas.

"Yes, I used to play tennis. But my arthritis bothers me. Just play a set of doubles now and then. The membership did help my business," replied Vir.

"How so?" asked Vas.

"Socialize over dinner and drinks and then discuss business," said Vir.

"Interesting," observed Vas.

"What about Meena?" asked Nalini.

"She plays bridge with the wives of my business contacts," siad Vir.

"Meena, do you enjoy it?" asked Nalini.

"Yes, I do. They have elected me as chair of the social committee."

"Vir, Was your dad a member of any club back in India?" asked Padmini.

"As a judge he was offered honorary membership, but he declined."

"I wonder why!"

"Because he thought there was a conflict. In case any of them appeared before him," explained Vir.

"I remember he was very strict and principled. Still remember the photocopies he made for our Golconda trip and underlined some important passages about Hindu-Muslim relations," recalled Prabu.

"Yes, he belonged to another time and generation. Not practical anymore," said Vir.

"Why would you say that?" queried Ramu.

"Well, Sharia law in a Hindu country is not practical. It also forbids family planning," said Vir.

"Lack of family planning is also related to poverty and lack of education. This would be the same for Hindus as well," said Ramu.

"I don't agree," shot back Vir.

"The Census Bureau does not confirm the view that muslims will outnumber Hindus," said Vas.

"But there are projections to the contrary," insisted Vir.

"That will not happen in a hundred years," chuckled Vas.

"Don't be so smug," interjected Roop.

"But Vir, I don't remember you being dogmatic back in the day. Now you seem very active in the temple," remarked Vas.

"Yes, we are very involved. We need to uphold our faith. How about you?" asked Vir.

"I have not changed much. Believe in a higher force and say a prayer at home," replied Vas.

"You said Hindus and Muslims in India are more religious now. Why is that?"

"It has just happened. Religion is the glue that binds them. We have more temples and mosques than schools and hospitals. *Allahu Akbar* has become louder and temple *ghantas* stronger."

"Sounds like a competition. So, what's going to happen?" asked Roop.

"Well, more conflict and clashes," replied Vas in a dejected tone.

"Perhaps it is time to ban all religions and have one unified world religion," Ramu proposed.

"That could lead to another world war," chuckled Prabu.

"What do you think of the leaders in India today?" asked Vir.

"Well, I don't see a Gandhi or Maulana Azad in the firmament," responded Vas in a regretful tone.

"Screw them," snapped Roop. "They have messed up our country."

"Shh. Enough. It's time to leave," Madhuri checked him, creeping up from behind.

To break the conversation, Meena summoned the six friends to pose in front of their mansion for a picture. Vir and Roop made their way together to the center, flanked by Prabu and Patel on one side and Vas and Ramu on the other. This configuration seemed to form naturally. Then there were pictures of the individual couples and finally the housekeeper was sent to capture the image of the entire group.

They headed to the same two cars and occupied the same seats. As they heard the sound of ignition spark the engine, Vas seemed engrossed in deep thought. He felt like a detached observer looking at a world that was surreal. Familiar images of the past seemed to fade and lacked in relevance. It was as if old memories were no longer important and were just an aberration. He felt a sense of loss, even sadness. A memory that was shared had now become his own to keep. A burden of sorts that he alone would have to carry.

Then he was overcome with doubt. Was he a sentimental old fool who had made too much of things of the past? A hopeless romantic? Maybe he was wrong, and the others were right. Maybe he was a dreamer and an idealist who could not adjust to new reality.

A formal table of twelve awaited them at the country club. The club was located in the north end of the city in a secluded woody area. Far from the madding crowd, it was established on a forty-five-acre plot of farmland in the county some hundred years earlier, by rich businessmen for other businessmen." The trees bore marks made by native Indians to identify the trails used by them in their treks from Detroit to Saginaw.

Founding members were mostly white Anglo-Saxons. Access to the exclusive club was restricted to those who met the strict criteria! Over the years, rich Jewish doctors and businessmen managed to gain entry.

Black people, Chinese folks, and Indians were among the last to be accepted, provided they were sponsored by members who were of good standing. Vir was among only a few South Asians to earn the privilege twenty years earlier.

The club was floundering then, with a drop in memberships due to racial and social insensitivities. A junior white business partner of his sponsored him and attested to his character and professional standing. He vouched for his ability to afford the membership fees. A formal interview followed with an all-white committee. It felt like a ritual of passage to mark a major social milestone in his life. He was well prepared. They were satisfied and recommended him to the board of directors after checking his credentials and credit ratings. Vir was delighted when he received the letter from the president of the board congratulating him on his successful application. He was as excited as he was decades ago when he received the congratulatory letter from the dean of the engineering college in Hyderabad on his admission. He had cracked a new barrier in a foreign land. He was a trailblazer who had cut through racial red tape. Now he was among people of power and influence.

The initiation fee was fifty thousand dollars. He could easily afford it. He enjoyed golf in his younger years and played on the nine-hole course which was extended to an eighteen-hole in the mid-nineties. Invitational tournaments brought in the likes of the Golden Bear and other golf legends. He was delighted to shake their hands and get their autographs.

There were also tennis and squash courts that he used in his younger years. An Olympic-sized swimming pool was added at the turn of the century. They took their daughter Preeti for swimming lessons. There were casual as well as formal dining areas and other amenities that they enjoyed.

Vir and Meena tiptoed around the club in the initial years, not wanting to make any mistakes or slip up on etiquette. They grew in confidence steadily. Now they were comfortably ensconced. They skated the club social rink fluidly.

Vir was also able to write off part of the membership as related to his professional expenses as he used the venue to discuss business. He entertained them in the dining hall. Things had gotten tighter with the IRS in recent years, but he was able to justify things through some creative accounting.

Meena was initially considered a guest of her husband and an adornment. She had gotten to know many of the ladies through bridge, tennis, and social events. Through the gossip mill, she learned that the spouses' membership could become a bone of contention when their marriages unravelled. Their lawyers had to fight it out to save their membership. It got even more complicated when they remarried. It meant a second initiation fee! However, this did not concern her, as her marriage was rock-solid. The Judge had indeed matched them brilliantly.

The country club meant prestige and status to Vir and Meena. It was a world they stepped into to escape the tedium and mundane of daily life. The expensive lifestyle of leisure, the sporting activities, and socializing with people of wealth and influence appealed to them. Vir enjoyed the sporting amenities until his knees gave out a few years back. Now he mostly enjoyed the social part of club life.

As they made their way through the halls to the dining area, the group began to take in the atmosphere. The ambience was elegant and formal. The dining hall was impressive with cherry wood dining tables and matching chairs spaced optimally to afford privacy as well as limited conversation between adjacent tables. There was a large stone fireplace at the north end of the room which emitted a warm and toasty glow. An old-fashioned Georgian clock above the mantelpiece had faithfully kept time since the opening of the club. Vas and Savitri were struck by the crystal chandeliers, portraits of distinguished members, original painting of the club building at the time of inception, art work in water colours, and golf memorabilia signed by famous golfers like Ben Hogan and Arnold Palmer.

The table was laid formally. The setting was resplendent with fine porcelain, sparkling crystal, gleaming silver, and rich linen. Vas and Patel cringed with nervousness as they eyed the elaborate cutlery around the dinner plates. They didn't know what utensil to use for which course. They were afraid of embarrassing themselves and their host. Their memory conjured up scenes from the Peter Sellers movie where he portrays an Indian making a fool of himself in a party.

As they sat down, Meena sensed their discomfort and whispered, "Just start on the outside and work your way in. The fork and knife closest to the plate is for the main course."

Mohini and Nalini took this as a cue and followed her movements.

The waiter, a white man in his fifties, in a purple jacket and green club tie showed up. He displayed a bronze custom name tag with the name "Jack," and introduced himself. There was an air of familiarity between him and Vir.

"Mr. Sri . . . vaas . . . tava," he said. "Good evening."

"Good evening Jack. Meet my classmates from school in India. From the sixties, would you believe?"

"Gentlemen, welcome. What a great reunion."

"Indeed. I am meeting them after many decades," confirmed Vir.

"Lovely. I hope you are enjoying our beautiful county and lovely weather."

"Very much so, thank you," said Roop, on behalf of everyone.

"How long are you here for?"

"Just the long weekend. We are off on Monday," responded Roop.

"May I offer you a drink? What can I get you?" He went round the table taking their orders. Savitri and Vas ordered fresh orange juice.

"I will be back with your drinks," Jack replied and walked away.

Everyone seemed a little nervous as they considered the menu options. To break the ice, Roop asked Vir what amenities he enjoyed in the club.

"An occasional game of tennis doubles. You know, my knees are bad. I may go for a replacement. Meena enjoys the bridge with the ladies."

The Reunion

A few ladies walked by and greeted Meena. "These are Vir's classmates from India," she said.

"Hello. Welcome to Michigan." Turning to Padmini, one of the ladies remarked, "What a gorgeous outfit! I love the brilliant colours."

"It's an Indian *saree*," Meena answered.

"Wow, I love it. Do you have any, Meena?"

"Loads. But I hardly wear it. Not convenient, you know. I wear it only when we go to our temple."

"I understand. You should wear it for our annual ladies' dinner."

"Will do." She glanced at Vir for approval.

The waiter returned with the drinks and took the orders. Ramu discussed the available options on behalf of the vegetarians. The waiter offered to remove the meat from the non-vegetarian offerings if they wished. There were no takers.

The food arrived and they proceeded cautiously, choosing the right utensil for the right dish. They exchanged glances to make sure they were coordinating their moves.

Vir asked Roop, "So, how are things in Georgia?"

"Fine. We belong to a club as well. Both Madhuri and I play golf. She won the ladies' league tournament last year."

"That's amazing."

"They spoil us. Bring the cart out with our clubs before the round and store it afterwards. Clean our shoes and clubs after the game. Our golf balls are monogrammed," said Roop gloatingly.

"They do that here, too," reacted Vir.

Ramu and Prabu listened passively, as if they were eying a showroom display from outside an expensive store.

Patel and Nalini enjoyed the meal and the experience. They seemed quite Indifferent to the impression they were making or not making.

Prabu and Mohini seemed secure in the social vortex they had created for themselves. They interacted with each other through their eyes and uttered as few words as possible.

After the meal, Vir showed them around the amenities, greeting friends as he encountered them. He seemed supple in his movements, as if gliding effortlessly on a social sheet of ice.

As they walked towards the car, he met his friend Rick.

"Hi Rick, meet my classmates from India."

"Honoured to meet you," said Rick. "How long are you here for?"

"Just the weekend," replied Vas.

"Have you done much sightseeing?"

"Yes, we've seen the town as well as the temple. Mostly we've been spending time together."

"Vir, you should take them to the Ford Museum. They will like the antique cars and get to know our American history," suggested Rick.

"Yes, I am thinking of taking them tomorrow while Meena takes the girls for a mani-pedi spa."

"Happy July fourth," greeted Rick.

"Same to you," replied Vir. "We are lucky to live in this great country."

"The best country in the world," crowed Rick.

The Reunion

"I agree. We have lived the American dream." Pointing to Ramu and Prabu, Vir added, "These two guys are from Canada. I am pursuading them to move to the USA."

"Won't be necessary if they become our fifty-first state," Rick giggled..

"Ha ha," chuckled Vir.

Ramu and Prabu looked on impassively.

"This guy here is from England," said Vir pointing to Patel.

"God save the Queen's country," mocked Rick.

Patel ignored the comment and stretched out his hand to greet him.

"What's your line of work?" asked Rick.

"I am in the jewelry business," replied Patel.

"Will Brexit help?"

"There's a lot of uncertainty. We import a lot from Europe, so with Brexit it will be difficult," responded Patel.

"Did you vote for Brexit?" asked Rick.

"No. Like your President, Boris doesn't have a clue. He is just whipping up nationalist feelings. Not good for new immigrants."

"But Brexit will stop illegal immigration, won't it?" pressed Rick.

"Also legal immigration, if you are not white," gibed Patel.

"We have a real problem at our southern border," continued Rick.

Patel ignored the comment and withdrew.

Turning to Vir, Rick asked, "By the way, are you coming to the fundraiser at David's?"

"Yes, we will be there," confirmed Vir.

"You know the Dems are out there with the voter registration drive," cautioned Rick.

"Yes, they are working hard to get the black vote out."

"We need to line up with the evangelicals," Rick added.

"I agree. I am trying to get the Hindus in the temple to vote for him. Trump and Modi are having a joint event in a few weeks. The tickets are selling like hotcakes," responded Vir.

"I hear Indians love Trump," commented Rick.

"Yes, they do. Because he is patriotic like their leader," said Vir.

"The president is also taking on China. I think it's about time," Roop joined in the conversation.

"Indians don't trust them either. They invaded our country after their Prime Minister said we are 'like brothers" in the sixties," added Vir.

"Anyways I won't hold you up. We can chat tomorrow. Nice meeting you all," Rick said as he was leaving.

"By the way I have invited a few of my Indian and American friends to meet my guests.. Why don't you and Julie join us for lunch tomorrow?" invited Vir.

"That will be wonderful. We will be there, thank you. Anything we can bring?" asked Rick.

"Just your sense of humour!" replied Vir.

The others looked on with deadpan expressions. Rick and Vir shook hands and parted.

Back in the car, Vas heaved a sigh of relief. A sense of aloofness descended on him. He retreated into himself. Another spell of silence hung between them. He was thinking of the day of departure.

The Reunion

On the way back home, Vir drove to the park across the city hall to see the July Fourth fireworks. It was a brilliant display of colours and formations, one surpassing the other and shooting up into the sky. The grand finale of the evening came when the American flag unfurled in the sky out of the glitter of a shooting star. The gathering of about a thousand burst into applause and started singing the star-spangled banner. Meena, Madhuri, Vir, and Roop, stood up and joined the chorus with their right hand over their heart. Their visitors got up and gazed at the sky in wonderment.

As they parted for the night, Vir popped a general question, to no one in particular. "Hope you guys enjoyed the evening?"

Roop answered, "Yes, it was a lot of fun, thank you."

"How about you ladies?" Meena gently probed.

"It was wonderful," Madhuri responded. All the others nodded in agreement.

Before they headed back to their rooms, Vir said he would drive the boys to the Ford Museum after lunch the next day. They retired for the night. There was another busy day ahead.

The next morning, Vir took his friends for a walk in the neighborhood while the ladies sat on the patio deck, enjoying their coffee.

"Does your son like it in Seattle?" Madhuri asked Mohini.

"Yes, they both work for Microsoft. They drive over to Vancouver to see us at least once every two weeks. What about your son, Anoop? You said he is in St Francisco."

"He is good. Still single. Doesn't want to get married," Madhuri said with a sense of disappointment.

"Why is that?" asked Mohini.

"Not met the right girl, I imagine." replied Madhuri.

"He lives on the other coast. Do you visit him there?"

"No. He prefers to meet us at our place in Georgia."

"So, he has not yet found a girl he likes?" asked Mohini.

"I am not sure. I don't think so," replied Madhuri.

"Have you tried to arrange a match?" asked Mohini.

"No, he strictly forbids it," responded Madhuri.

"Maybe he is shy of girls," commented Mohini.

"A little. As a little boy he played with dolls, while Arun liked toy trucks."

"What about as a teenager?" enquired Mohini.

"He was a little aloof and timid. He would come home from school crying at times. Roop would ask why, but he would never tell," recalled Madhuri.

"Did he go to the school prom?"

"No he skipped it," replied Madhuri.

Inserting herself into the conversation, Meena said, "My friend Jane in the club said their son recently announced he is gay."

"But my son Anoop is not gay. He is just not interested in marriage. How did Jane and her parents react?" asked Madhuri.sounding interested.

"Their hearts broke. They are hoping it is a phase and he will get over it," replied Meena.

"Will they accept him if he doesn't?" questioned Madhuri.

"They keep saying he is their pride and joy . . . but . . ."

"But what?" asked Nalini.

"They are strict Christians. They think it is a sin," explained Meena.

The Reunion

"Is that what the Bible says?" asked Nalini.

"Yes. Marriage is between Adam and Eve, not Adam and Steve!" replied Meena.

"So how are your friends going to deal with their son?" asked Madhuri.

"Their pastor told them all will be well if he turns to Jesus. He said it can be cured," answered Meena.

"Do you think he will heed the pastor's advice?" asked Madhuri.

"No, he has flatly refused. He told his parents it's not a disease to cure," said Meena.

"Back in India, we never heard about this gay business," Nalini interjected.

"But the *Kamasutra* devotes an entire chapter to homosexual behaviour," Padmini added, entering the conversation.

"You think we have always had gay people in India?" asked Nalini curiously.

"Yes, but only inside closed doors. We are not a gay friendly country," explained Padmini.

"What about now? Are Indians more open to the idea? Nalini asked.

"Yes, much better. The Supreme Court of India has made gay relationships legal," informed Padmini.

"Will that allow them to be more open, like here?" Nalini wanted to know.

"Better maybe but not totally. Both Hindu and Muslim clerics are against it. They believe marriage is made of man and woman. Not man and man, or woman and woman."

"That's what my friend Jane says," said Meena.

"Baba Namdev said homosexuality is an addiction and can be cured through yoga," Padmini added.

"Is that possible?" asked Madhuri.

"His followers believe it is possible," responded Padmini.

"Anyway, we hope your son finds a girl soon," reassured Nalini, turning to Madhuri.

"I am sure he will," she replied.

Vir took his friends on a walk to the cul-de-sac which had the largest homes. It was eerily silent. No one could be seen. Vas wondered where they were and thought of the busy street he lived on. He could hear its constant ebb and flow from oceans away.

"It is safe and quiet here," Vir said.

"Too quiet for me," countered Vas.

"I can't handle the sound pollution in India anymore."

"For me, the silence here is too loud."

"But it is so clean here. No garbage on the street," Vir said.

"That's correct. We have to improve our civic sense," admitted Vas

"Will that ever happen?" asked Roop.

"Well, that is the question. Even people who visit foreign countries behave the same after returning home," responded Vir with a sense of lament in his tone.

Meena set up a buffet lunch for the afternoon. The table was set with plates and serviettes, forks and knives, cups and glasses. The Taj Indian Restaurant catered for this informal event. Everyone looked relaxed, unlike the previous evening. The menu consisted of *Tandoori* chicken, vegetable *biryani, naan*, *dal makhani*, *aloo gobi*, *raita* and *papadams*. They were served vegetable *samosas* for appetizers.

They didn't have to worry about cutlery. They could let their guard down. Vas and Ramu

were relieved that the vegetarian dishes were demarcated from the non vegetarian dishes by twelve inches of separation. They were uncomfortable when serving spoons were used interchangeably.

Vir's neighbours, Rick and Julie, arrived first, followed by Steve and Susan. Later, their Indian friends joined. Rick spotted Ramu and Prabu and headed towards them. Vir took orders for drinks. Meena supervised the table as the girls appointed themselves to different roles.

"So how are things back home in India?" asked Steve.

"We both live in Canada," said Prabu.

"Yes, I remember from yesterday. Do you have family in India?" asked Steve.

"Cousins and extended family," said Prabu.

"We hear India is doing great economically, but there is a lot of poverty still."

"That's true. We have a thriving middle class," said Ramu.

"And a lot of the super rich. Vir told me about Ambani. One of the richest people in the world."

"He belongs to my community," Patel piped in.

"Which community is that?" asked Rick.

"We are *gujaratis*, the business community. Modi comes from our community," replied Patel.

"Mahatma Gandhi, too," added Ramu.

"Is the caste system still practised in India?" asked Steve.

"Yes, but things are slowly improving," replied Prabu.

"How do you know?"

"I am myself from the backward class," replied Prabu.

"Oh, I am sorry. I was not aware."

"Don't be. We can still talk about it," said Prabu.

"Did you face a lot of discrimination in India?" enquired Steve.

"My father felt it more than I. He was a *peon*."

"What's a *peon*?" asked Rick.

"A low-ranking office job. Simple tasks. Mostly drudge work."

"But you became a doctor?"

"Yes. There was a quota that I qualified for."

"Sounds like affirmative action for Black people here," posited Rick.

"May be. Yours is based on race. Ours is based on caste."

"Yes, Black discrimination goes back to the time of slavery," stated Rick. "That is a few hundred years old."

"How old is the caste system?" asked Rick.

"Thousands of years. It was intended as an occupational division but slowly morphed into discrimination based on lineage," explained Prabu.

"Do you think affirmative action in India has lasted too long as in America?" asked Steve.

"I don't think so, because discrimination continues to exist. They are still stigmatized, perhaps like African Americans in the USA," responded Ramu.

"But the white working class folk have also been left behind," said Steve.

"Is that because they are white?" asked Vas.

"Yes. As if they have to pay for the sins of their forefathers," said Steve questioningly..

"Shouldn't they?" asked Vas.

"I am not sure, what do you think?" retorted Steve.

"It is an ethical question," said Vas.

"How do Indians feel about this," asked Rick.

"There is some backlash to the quota system in India as well," replied Vas.

"Will the quota system survive in India?" asked Rick.

"In the public sector, yes, but it is being opposed by the private sector. The corporate world can set its own hiring policies," replied Vas.

"Has the plight of Black people improved in America?" queried Prabu.

"The Black middle class has definitely grown here due to AA in education and jobs," replied Steve.

"That's good, isn't it?" probed Prabu gently.

"Yes, but we need to help the white working class as well. They have fallen behind," maintained Steve.

"What does 'Make America Great Again' really mean?" asked Ramu.

"It is a call to patriotism," replied Steve.

"Is that patriotism or nationalism?" asked Ramu.

"Is there a difference?" questioned Steve.

"I think so. Patriots believe in shared values. Nationalists believe in a shared culture," clarified Ramu.

Vas interposed, "I heard that MAGA is a secret code for MAWA."

"And what's that?" asked Rick.

"Make America White Again."

"Well, I don't think so. Ask Vir. I am sure he feels as much an American as I," said Rick.

"I hope he does," replied Vas.

Prabu then walked towards the buffet and surveyed the table before filling his plate. The others followed. Prabu, Ramu, Vas, and Patel were then joined by Vir's Indian friends, Ram and Amar. They introduced themselves as old friends and business associates of Vir's. They too had retired recently and were active in the temple.

"Do you visit India?" Vas inquired.

"Yes, in the winter months. I have a flat in Bangalore in an NRI gated community," Ram answered.

"Do you enjoy it?"

"Yes, very much. The enclave is very private. All modern amenities," said Ram.

"Do any locals live there?" asked Prabu.

"Just the rich Indians who work in the city. They treat it as a getaway cottage on weekends," replied Ram.

"What do you think of India now?" asked Vas.

"Great progress. Modi is the right man for our country," said Amar.

"Like Trump here?" asked Patel.

"Yes, they are both the right men for the right job at the right time," Amar stated categorically.

"Don't minorities in both countries feel under siege," asked Vas.

"On the contrary, Muslims in India are better off than in any other Muslim country. Especially muslim women have more freedoms," said Amar.

The Reunion

"That is because we are a democratic country and the Muslim countries are not," said Vas.

"But that doesn't mean we have to lose our Hindu identity," asserted Ram.

"Our identity is secure. We have nothing to fear," said Vas.

"We can't take it for granted. History warns us that medieval invasions have destroyed our culture," continued Ram.

"Historically, India has embraced different cultures and has been a melting pot similar to the U.S.," said Vas.

"But the glue is running out of the melting pot," said Ram sarcastically.

"Aren't you concerned that the anti- minority sentiment in the U.S. is bad for Indians as it is for Muslims in India?" asked Prabu.

"No. Our minority is safe here," said Ram.

"How can you be so sure?" persisted Prabu.

"We are an educated and affluent minority group." answered Ram.

"Does that protect us from hate crimes?" questioned Prabu.

"Those incidents are rare," argued Ram.

"So, do you think we should forsake pluralism in India?" asked Vas.

"Yes, we have run too far with that. Time to roll it back," said Amar.

"Will your children and grandchildren be safe here as they don't look like whites?" asked Vas.

"I am sure they will be," remarked Amar.

"So, you feel safe voting for Trump again," asked Vas.

"Absolutely. The democrats and the congress party in India have sold us out. Do you vote for the Congress Party?" asked Amar.

"I am not for the Congress Party either. I don't vote at all. I don't trust any politicians."

Vas then excused himself and walked towards his wife Savitri. "Are you ok?"

"Yes. I am ready to go home," she said.

"Me too!" he agreed.

Roop and Madhuri were in conversation with Steve and Susan in the other corner of the room. Vas overheard Roop saying, "We need to work hard from now on to next November as Georgia is up for grabs."

Steve said, "But Georgia has always voted Republican."

"Not this time. It is turning purple. The Dems are concentrating on the Black turn out."

"Same here in Michigan," said Vir, joining them. "And Biden is sure to roll back the tax cuts."

"Our stocks are going to fall after that great Trump ride," Steve feared.

"We hear he may be in trouble with the law if he loses," Vir posited.

"My psychiatrist colleagues think he is a creative hustler and will get the better of them, besides, Trumpism will prevail even after he is gone," reassured Roop.

"That's what we are going to need to counter socialism," Steve concluded.

Ramu and his wife Padmini were locking horns with Aruna and Uma. "We hear Trudeau welcomed nearly 25,000 refugees from the Middle East recently" Aruna said.

"We call it the policy of multuculturalism," responded Padmini.

"Who pays for the refugee programmes?"

"The government provides them with an initial financial loan which they pay back," said Padmini.

"Isn't that unfair, as it comes out of your taxes initially,?" said Aruna.

"Maybe. But, overall it contributes to the economy and builds a healthy multicultural community which is good for everyone," explained Padmini.

"It is different here. American exceptionalism is based on individualism," retorted Aruna.

"Canadian exceptionalism—there, I just coined a new phrase—is based on communitarianism," answered Aruna.

Fortunately, they saw Meena approaching them for dessert. Their conversation ended.

The guests began to leave. Everyone shook hands bidding their bye byes.

"It was a pleasure meeting you," echoed through the room multiple times. It sounded a little hollow.

"I need to go and pack," said Nalini.

"Wait a minute, I have something for you all," said Meena and hurried up to her room. She came down with the picture of the gang she had taken on the front porch before the country club dinner. She had made a quick trip to IKEA to have them framed. The boys were delighted at her thoughtfulness. They gave her a warm hug to show their appreciation and thanked both her and Vir for their hospitality. Vir told them to rest up for a bit.

After tea, he drove the boys to the Ford Museum about an hour away. This was a large history museum that the boys loved. They were thrilled to see the JFK presidential limousine. They admired the president growing up back in the sixties and were in awe of him. They also saw the chair that Lincoln sat in at the Ford Theater before he was assassinated. The Rosa Parks bus reminded them of the conversation they had had earlier about the blacks. They especially loved the antique cars from the first Model T to the A, the Mustang, and the vintage cars. The horse-drawn carriages and old cars reminded Vir and Roop of the jalopies their parents used to own. That seemed ages ago.

This last trip was like a breath of fresh air. It was the perfect ending for a less than perfect reunion. It was free from conflict and controversy. It brought out the kids in them. An apt reminder of their virgin days of innocence.

And then it happened.

As Vir cruised home in the van with Roop by his side, Ramu and Prabu behind, and Patel and Vas in the last row, he noticed the red and blue flashing lights in the rear view mirror. His heart sank with a sick feeling in his stomach. He realized immediately what had happened. He had exceeded the speed limit. The speedometer read eighty miles per hour. It was a seventy miles per hour zone. He started slowing down. Soon the siren and flashing lights were right behind him.

He turned on the indicator signal to the right and stopped the van on the hard shoulder. There was an eerie quiet in the car. Vas was jolted out of a brief nap at the back. The officer parked his car with the lights on and approached the

The Reunion

van. The burly, six-foot-tall, white officer in a blue uniform stood outside the driver side. He seemed well muscled with broad shoulders. He had a stern and humourless face. The silver shaped badge with an enamel finish shimmered on his chest. It added a sense of authority to his countenance. Vas was petrified, drops of sweat forming on his temples. He had never seen such a large cop up close.

"Sir you were ten miles over the limit," he informed in a commanding tone.

"I'm very sorry, Officer," Vir replied.

"Do you have any firearms in the car?" the officer asked sternly.

"No, Sir," Vir replied meekly.

"May I see your ownership and insurance documents?"

"Sure, here they are," replied Vir nervously gathering the documents from the glove box.

"Who are these people in the car?"

"My classmates from school."

"What are they doing here?"

"They are visiting me. We are having a class reunion."

"Where are they from?" interrogated the officer.

"One next to me is from the USA, the two behind are from Canada, and in the last row, one is from UK and the other is from India," Vir replied in a shaky voice.

"Sir, I need to see all their IDs. Can you both in the front seats step out of the car and stand by the side there with your hands behind your heads while I check your documents. The others remain in the car."

Vir and Roop obeyed his instructions.

The officer stepped aside and spoke to someone on his walkie talkie. Soon another cop arrived.

The second officer ordered the remaining four passengers to exit the vehicle and instructed them to stand in another corner. He told them to keep their hands behind their heads while he checked their documents.

They were ordered back into the van by the two officers one after the other.

Finally, the officer approached Vas. "Sir, where are you from?"

"Hyderabad," replied Vas nervously.

"Hy . . .de . . .ra..bad? Where the fuck is that?"

"India, sir," replied Vas, his face pale and perspiring.

"I need to see your driver's licence," he demanded.

"Sorry, sir. I don't drive in India, so I don't have a driver's licence."

"How do you get around there?"

"I have a car and a driver there," replied Vas.

"Oh, a big shot, are we?" the Officer said mockingly.

"No sir. Most people have drivers there."

"Hmm. In that case I need to see your passport," the Officer stated.

"My passport is with my wife at my friend's house," explained Vas.

"I am afraid I can't release you until I see it," the Officer told Vas.

"Sir, please, I have a valid visa to visit America."

"That's not good enough. I need to see it. Where is your friend's house?" the Officer insisted.

"I can't remember his address. It's in the county close by. Please ask my friend who is driving the van. I am staying with him," pleaded Vas.

"Well I will ask your friend to have your wife meet us at the county police station with both your passports. You go stand by my cruiser with your hands behind your head. I will join you momentarily," the Officer ordered Vas.

"Sir, please let me go with them," pleaded Vas.

"Do not argue, sir. Do as you are told."

Vas steadied himself as his legs weakened. He almost fell backwards while holding his hands behind his head waiting for the officer to return.

The officer walked to the van and explained the plan to Vir. The other officer handed him a citation with two demerit points and a fine of two hundred dollars. Vir accepted the verdict without a whisper.

He then pleaded, "Officer, please let my friend come in the car. We will meet you at the police station. My wife will drive my friend's wife with the passports to the station." .

"No, sir. You follow my orders and drive home. I will bring your friend to the police station. You have his wife meet us at the station with the passports."

Vir did as he was told and turned on the ignition.

As they drove out, they saw the officer handcuff Vas before shoving him in the back of the police car.

Vas began to shiver uncontrollably in the cruiser. He had no idea what was going to happen to him. Whether they would throw him and Savitri in jail. In all his seventy plus years he had never experienced anything like this.

He felt frightened and humiliated. Violated and disgraced. Unclean and tainted. Made to look like a common criminal. He closed his eyes and started praying. That he would be set free and return to Hyderabad on the next flight.

Savitri froze when she saw her husband in shackles. With tears in her eyes, she handed the passports to the officer. He inspected the documents and scanned it. Fortunately, he was satisfied and released him.

With a gleeful smile, he added, "Enjoy the reunion," and returned the documents.

When they returned home, Vas embraced Savitri. They then broke down.

Vir had nothing to say about what had happened. Roop gave Vas and Savitri a sleeping tablet and the two went up to bed. It was stone quiet before they all made their way to their bedrooms.

The next morning was a new day. They were packed and ready to leave. They bid their final goodbyes. As they parted, Prabu became quite emotional and began to sob. He was overwhelmed by events, especially of the last evening. The boys surrounded him to console him with a tear or two in their own eyes.

"He has been like this since his heart attack," whispered Mohini to the ladies.

Vas was numb to the emotion of the moment. He was unmoved.

We should do this again," said Vir.

"I can host you all next time," said Roop.

The offer gained little traction and escaped into thin air. Then they left.

CHAPTER 16
The Homecoming

Is all well if it ends well?
Who must decide?

Vas was on his long flight back to India. Savitri seated next to him had gone to sleep. He could not turn off the images of the last few days. Especially of the horrific incident that dishonoured him. He began to understand why the immigration forces were called "Ice Agents." What they did to him was chilling. It stripped him of the dignity that he had guarded for years. He felt defiled and disfigured. Disgraced. His heart raced at the very thought of it. Optimism had been his greatest virtue, but not anymore.

Reputation, he realized, is fragile. He couldn't make sense of Vir and Roop either. How they could not be affected by what happened to him. Why were they so silent?

Why couldn't they protect him? It could have been them or their children or even their grandchildren. There was something deeper at play. How safe were they in a world that was changing precipitately?

He felt lucky to be leaving. The irony was not lost on him that Hyderabad was a safer haven by comparison. A sanctuary city!

Vir and Meena, he imagined, would return to their predictable lives, their politics, and their friends. Roop and Madhuri would similarly return to theirs in Georgia. They would campaign for Trump and vote for him a second time. They were in denial of the harsh reality that he endured firsthand. Admitting this was not an option, as they had run too far with it.

Ramu, he imagined would return to Toronto and Prabu to Vancouver. And Patel and Nalini would go home to their life in Birmingham. He wasn't sure what the reunion meant to each of them or even to himself. It is supposed to be the return of a group of people to a place they regarded as home. This was not that, as they met in a foreign land. In some ways it was like going on a honeymoon. To an exotic place to celebrate a friendship of fifty-five years. To enjoy and cherish old memories. There was certainly a sense of joyful anticipation before they met. They would catch up, reminisce, and celebrate old times. But once they met, a tussle between the past and present seemed to ensue. There was hurt and anger as it did not live up to expectations. The present seemed to have won out. Political differences became hard to bridge and posed a difficult barrier to overcome. Like the red and blue families in America who were at odds.

Can people align with one another, despite having differing core values? That was the question. When friendships are lost, they can seldom be found. He wondered if he was alone in dealing with this variance. There was some comfort in knowing that he was headed back home to familiar faces and friends. He was grateful.

He had a new appreciation for a city he knew well. A secure place where he could be himself. This was the place where his memories were made. Where he had hoped and dreamed.

"You can take me out of Hyderabad, but can't take Hyderabad out of me." Was that just a hackneyed cliche? Would it apply equally to Vir and Prabu, and Ramu and Patel? They were back in homes that were far away from their homes in Hyderabad. They had been taken out of Hyderabad, and much of Hyderabad had been taken out of them. Ramu and Prabu lived in Canada, a country they said encouraged integration. This meant they could keep their culture and yet be part of the whole. That they were equal to all others who were part of this whole. Were they? Were they being Canadian enough? Who were they really? Indo-Canadians or Canadian Indians? Were these trade-offs negotiable?

For Vir and Roop, Vas thought, the conflicts seemed less of an issue. They seemed to have blended completely into the tapestry. An assimilation. A tapestry of different coloured threads that had faded into one. They conformed to a narrative that did not tolerate conflict. Was this a Faustian bargain? What place did Hyderabad have in this mosaic?

The trite cliche "You don't know who you are until you know who you were," seemed on the surface at least, not to apply to them, as who they were had less likeness to who they had become. Like two chapters of the same book, unrelated and in different time zones.

Patel was less concerned about these matters. He seemed the freest of all. Ironically, he was no different than the British in the way he adjusted to a new country. The "Little India" he belonged to in Birmingham was similar to the "Little Britain" the Brits had created for themselves. They had transplanted a piece of their home all over India. In many ways he was the "True Son" of the Hyderabad soil, as he had never left it. He was more of a Hyderabadi than himself. Lately he questioned how much of Hyderabad was even left in Hyderabad!

Patel had managed to recreate "a slice of India" in a foreign land. Integration or assimilation mattered little to him. He was free as he could be himself. Like the British in India who had transplanted a piece of home in Indian soil. The churches, the hill stations, the private clubs, the food, the fox hunts, the riding clubs, and so on. They, too, did not integrate, let alone assimilate. Patel, it seemed, had beaten them on their own turf!

He celebrated festivals like *diwali* as he would have in India, with festoons of flowers, *diyas* and crackers. When he went shopping, he bargained as he did back home. He ate in Indian restaurants, spoke in *gujarati*, ate *paan*, and crossed the street whenever it opened up rather than wait for the pedestrian signal. His memories of home were intact and indestructible. He seemed to have his feet firmly planted. Life was on his terms. Not negotiated.

Vas and Savitri arrived in Hyderabad in the wee hours of the next morning. Their son Arun was waiting for them in the arrivals. Their eyes turned moist as they saw him. They embraced each other warmly. Vas felt he was back where he belonged. He had always shared everything with his son. There were no secrets. But he was not ready to share the terrible incident with him. It was too shameful.

"How was the trip?" asked his son Arun.

"Good," he replied hesitantly.

"How are your classmates? Did they recognize you?" Arun asked.

"I think so. Not sure if I recognized them!" he answered with sarcasm.

"You mean you didn't recognize them physically?"

"No, I mean emotionally," Vas replied.

"They must have changed?" asked Arun.

"Yes and no. Some more than the others."

"Did they think you have changed?" asked Arun.

"I am not sure! I have now," replied Vas sadly.

Arun was puzzled.

"How are things here?" asked Vas.

"Same old, same old."

"Have they completed the road repair on our street?" asked Vas.

"Not really. They had to stop as there was a *bandh*."

"What was the *bandh* about?"

"For increase in wages for construction workers."

"Was there an incident to cause the *bandh*?"

"Yes, a few of the workers were arrested for 'breach of the peace.'"

"Any chance of a resolution?" asked Savitri.

"Well, I expect soon, as it is into the third week and contractors can't afford to stall," replied Arun.

"Let's hope so, for the sake of the poor strikers. How are Sneha and little Mina?" enquired Savitri.

"They are fine Ma. Mina is eager to see you both."

As Arun turned into their street, their driver Zafar spotted their car and opened the gate.

It was heartwarming to see his smiling face.

"*Salaam Saab,*" he said. "Hope you enjoyed the trip."

"Yes, Zafar, we did. How are you?"

"*Allah ka Shukar,*" he replied, and then unloaded the suitcases from the trunk and carried it inside.

Vas sat down in his easy chair and closed his eyes. It felt peaceful. Savitri was back in the kitchen making a cup of coffee. She felt as if she was back in control. She was the queen of her own castle. She could do things her own way. She was buoyant and walked with a spring in her step.

She opened the back door to take a peek. The garden welcomed her back with its familiar sights and smells. The jasmines were in full bloom and filled the air with fragrance. The plants appeared to have grown a little taller. The early morning dew had not dried up yet as the sun shone through the drops to make them sparkle like diamonds.

Outside, on the street, the early morning walkers were up going about their workout. The sound of the roadside vendors and the auto rickshaw honks was a sign that she was home. The memory of America and Canada was beginning to recede. She thought of her grandchildren. Her family was the essential part of her happiness.

Vas settled back into his routine as easily as inserting his foot into a well-worn shoe. He was back in touch with his coffee group. He shared the pictures with them and told them all about the trip, the places he had visited, and the parties they had had. He especially described Vir's huge house, the country club dinner, and their opulent lifestyle with a sense of pride. He also talked about the political discussions they had had without going into detail. But he stopped short of the terrible incident of his arrest. His friends discerned a "sense of lament" in his voice and tone. They did not ask why.

After a few days his mind wandered back. He tried to sort through the jumble of thoughts. To rearrange them. But found it confusing. He wasn't sure of himself anymore and where he belonged. He envied Patel's sense of surety. In a way, he envied Roop and Vir as well, as they seemed ensconced in their lives and lifestyles. This must come from unconditional surrender, he thought. To the pressures of one's place and peers.

He was envious of them. He was home and yet not quite so. He seemed in it but not of it. Adrift. Was this because he had also changed? He was no different from his friends abroad, as he, too, had lived in a "foreign land" of his own making. A world that existed only in his imagination. The Hyderabad he knew no longer existed. The places they had frequented and the streets they had roamed were gone. They were no longer recognizable as they were swept up by the tsunami of change. So were their memories.

Even if they had met in Hyderabad and not Michigan it would not have mattered. Both were equally alien. They were immigrants in both places. He wondered who the "keepers of childhood memories" are. And if they were worth keeping. Did they exist in reality, or were they a fantasy of our own construction? It didn't really matter.

What mattered was the here and now.

He then placed the black and white picture of the gang on the left of the mantelpiece and the recent colour photograph on the right.

He laid back in his easy chair and pondered on one and then the other. Then he stared into the space in between.

EPILOGUE

About seven months after the reunion, the coronavirus pandemic hit America, in February of 2020. It had originated in a Chinese wet market in Wuhan some three months earlier. The aphorism attributed to Lenin that, "There are decades when nothing happens and then there are weeks when decades happen," assumed a whole new meaning.

As the virus raged through countries and continents, it upended life everywhere and derailed economies. It was impartial in picking its victims. Princes and paupers alike fell a prey to it. It also affected social behaviour at the elemental level. Face masks and social distancing became the hallmarks of self protection. The World Health Organization declared it a global pandemic. People were dying all over the world, and comparisons were made to the Spanish Flu a hundred years earlier. Trump repeatedly blamed China for spreading the virus. At a campaign rally in February of 2020, he declared that with warmer weather the virus would vanish. He defied health expert recommendations and refused to wear a mask. He called it a sign of weakness. His supporters imitated his attitude and behaviour..

Vir and Roop attended the Fox town hall meeting when he said, "Everybody has to be calm. It's all going to work out." He predicted the economy would come roaring back. This reassured them and their friends. They believed in him implicitly and explicitly.

The mask became the most prized as well as the most despised piece of face wear around the world. While the majority heeded the advice of public health officials, many rejected it as unnecessary. Trump openly contradicted the dire prophecies made by health care experts and assured everyone that the virus would be vanquished. He had terse exchanges with the press whenever they confronted and challenged him. His supporters viewed preventative measures as an affront to their democratic rights and freedoms. By contrast, countries like China and Singapore enforced compliance by using the full force of the state. They had better results.

Both public and private health care systems around the world were stretched and strained. By the time elections rolled in nine months later, in November of 2020, the country was deeply divided. Thousands of Americans had died. The eyes of the world were on Tuesday the third day of November when America went to the polls. It was called the most consequential election of our time.

It was feared that if Trump won a second term, there would be more disruption to foreign policy and international order. Institutions of government would be further eroded, and democracy would be in decline. Freedom of the press and the rule of law would be under siege. The white nationalist movement would be emboldened. A conservative party with a nationalistic fringe would become a nationalistic party

The Reunion

with a conservative fringe. The Republican Party would lose its soul if it decided to ride his coattails again.

Ian Bassin, the executive director of Protect Democracy, posited metaphorically, "At the very top of a volcano, there are supposed to be a bunch of checks and balances that hold back the heat and force. But we have a Congress that has basically abdicated its congressional obligations of oversight of the executive, and an executive who openly claims to be the law. So, you've got the lava exploding out the top of the volcano." But Vir and Roop were undaunted. They were convinced that Trump was irreplaceable. If he was not re-elected, the borders would become porous, and law and order would break down. The country would be swamped by immigrants, and the "American way of life" would be threatened.

They were undismayed by the threats to minorities. They were convinced that as they were amongst the most educated and highest earning ethnic group in the USA, with a median income of one hundred thousand dollars, they were safe. They supported his platform of "free market with less regulation, reduced taxes, and immigration control.

Hate crimes against Sikhs and South Asians were on the rise. There were attacks on Indian temples, mosques, and synagogues. Trump placed a hold on H1-B visas, preventing young engineers from India to come to the US. Vir and Roop argued, "We can't have people compete for American jobs when there is so much unemployment here." This was another Trump narrative they acquiesced to.

Trump ads ran in Hindi, Gujarati, and other languages in cinema halls screening Bollywood films. Some of the Indian support shifted to Biden when he picked Kamala

Devi Harris, a biracial woman with a Jamaican father and a South Indian mother. But a large swath of Indians were resolute in their support for Trump. The friendship between Trump and Modi grew. They were both described by some observers as imperious. Huge arguments broke out in the Indian community between Trump and Biden supporters. Families were torn apart. The Indian community was microcosmic of the split of the American Family at large.

Vir and Roop attended the huge Modi rally in Houston. It was attended by fifty thousand Indians. The crowd went into an excited frenzy when the two leaders embraced. It seemed that the politics of India and America intersected and intertwined at that very moment. Old arguments were rekindled and the cultural divides were reopened.

This was evocative of the "divide and rule" policy of the British in India in the service of imperialism. In this case, it was in the service of Trumpism.

Vir and Roop watched the first presidential debate. They cheered whenever Trump landed a punch on Biden. They were quiet when Biden exposed his spectacular failure in controlling the virus. They believed that the moderator was biased against Trump by asking him tougher questions while giving Biden a free pass. They were impressed by his "law and order" message. They agreed that protests around the country against police violence needed to be curbed. Biden, they concluded was, "too old and weak" to be a strong president.

Trump lost the elections. Vir and Roop were disappointed and dismayed. While more than half the country celebrated, the other half was enraged. Trump convinced his followers that just as he had predicted, he lost the elections because it was stolen from him. Vir and Roop were among the majority of republicans who believed in his claim. This was despite overwhelming evidence to the contrary. Bipartisan courts across the country including the Supreme Court of the country rejected his demand to overturn the election result.

On January sixth, 2021, Trump made an impassioned speech to "Fight like hell. Or you won't have a country anymore." The crowd of his supporters then stormed the Capitol.

Vir and Roop were stunned. They were not sure how to react. Their initial reaction was one of shock. But they could not bring themselves to condemn him, partly because of a fear that it would anger their neighbours and fellow campaigners, and partly because they had come too far now to turn back. The democrats tried to impeach him for inciting the crowd, but they failed. Vir and Roop have decided to support him again in his latest bid to make a comeback in 2024.

Ramu and Prabu returned to Canada. Like the majority of Canadians, they rejoiced when Biden was elected. They were relieved that the warm relations between the two countries could be restored, tariffs lifted, and environmental concerns addressed.

The pandemic hit Canada brutally, and the borders were soon closed. Prabu and Ramu could not visit their children in the U.S. and they could not visit them. Justin Trudeau and his party were in the spotlight with a minority government.

They were satisfied with his handling of the COVID crisis, but dissatisfied due to an inordinate delay in getting the vaccines. Ramu lamented that "Trudeau had dropped the ball on the issue of vaccines." Canadians were, however, strongly in favour of the timely stimulus checks sent to suffering

Canadians. Ramu and Padmini continue to lead their simple lives in Toronto. Like millions of others, they are waiting for their second dose of the vaccine. They will then be able to travel to see their grandchildren across the border.

Prabu received his vaccine as he was on the priority list due to his health concerns. Mohini is waiting patiently for her second dose. Now in the twilight of his life journey, and having come close to dying, he considers himself much luckier than his poor father who had to live with the label of "backward class" hung around his neck like an albatross. He has felt much freer living abroad. He does not have to carry that cross anymore.

Caste, he explains to his white Canadian friends, is hard wired into the psyche of Indians. It influences their decisions and choices regarding friendships and associations. It is ubiquitous and transcends religion. It is present in varying degrees in Muslim and Christian communities as well. Each caste finds one that is inferior to its own to look down upon. Being at the "bottom of the heap," he exclaims, his community has felt the collective weight of all the ones above. He is, however, hopeful as things have changed. Policy changes, coupled with the new trend of inter-caste dating, is gradually breaking the mould. There is a rise in inter-caste marriages. There are not as many as one might hope, but it is an encouraging trend, nevertheless.

Patel and Nalini returned to their "predictable lives" in England. He is close to wrapping up the sale of his jewelry stores to another young *gujarati* entrepreneur in his forties. He reminds him of himself.

Back home in India, there has been a sea change. With a booming economy, attitudes have changed, and with it, the family structure. Urban families have turned nuclear and the average Indian family has shrunk from six members to four. Patel's family also splintered, and their joint family system dissolved. The family store established over a hundred years ago was closed and the inventory parceled among the cousins. They opened smaller branches all around the city. It was emblematic of the demise of a century old labour of love.

Elderly folk have been dislocated due to the sociological reset of the family system. Retirement homes have opened up everywhere. Parents of Indians abroad (NRIs) especially have moved into them as their children resided abroad. Patel's mother passed away, leaving his own father to move into a "home for the aged." His father preferred that to living with him in the UK, as he would not be able to adjust to the cold weather and constant rain.

Patel hopes to spend the winter months in Hyderabad after the sale of his business. He hopes to reconnect with his cousins as well as visit his father, who is now in his late eighties. He looks forward to spending time with Vas in Hyderabad. They will try to track Rashid down.

Vas and Savitri were back to their routines in Hyderabad. They returned to a politics which was radioactive. The new laws passed by the government have made religion a basis for citizenship. This has created divisions along familiar lines. While asylum claims of non-Muslims from neighbouring countries of Afghanistan, Bangladesh, and Pakistan have been fast-tracked, this has been denied to Muslim applicants. The government denies it is discriminatory and claims that these were Hindus who were not able to come to India at the time of partition in 1947. They say that they are righting an old wrong.

Indians of all faiths have protested against the law. Reading passages from the constitution, and reciting poems and songs have become popular expressions of dissent. Hindu supporters of Modi, on the other hand have endorsed the policy of the government. They believe that it is a legitimate piece of legislation.

There is thus an impasse.

The future of Hindu-Muslim relations in India is as uncertain as it has been in the past. The co-mingling of politics and religion is not a new phenomenon. Interactions between the two faiths have historically witnessed periods of conflict as well as cooperation. While the two

religions have coexisted, they have also striven to maintain their distinctiveness. Vas continues to impress on his group of friends that they are two different philosophical doctrines which are not poles apart. Despite the external differences, they have much in common and worship the same "Supreme Being."

Until this is understood, he laments, this relationship will continue to be imperfect and have ups and downs, like jagged edges that can be smoothed but not rounded.

These divisions are perhaps fueled by age-old narratives. There is a primeval fear among Hindus that if Muslims were to outnumber them, medieval Muslim rule will come to pass again. This conjures up dark images. The angst among Muslims is that if they capitulate, they might be overpowered and drowned in a sea of Hindus. The very same narratives that led to the partition, as Mr.Hussain, the history teacher, had explained many years ago. These are existential fears that have lasted over decades..

The Reunion

Rashid retired as a senior food scientist in the department of agriculture. Their three children are all married and emigrated to the USA. He and his wife Naima have moved into a retirement home in Hyderabad. He spends his time advising farmers about modern methods of irrigating crops and teaching the meaning of Quran to young children. He is a teacher like his father. His brother Karim never recovered from the forced break up of his affair with the Hindu girl. He never married. He wonders if he and his Hindu girl friend would have better luck today. He probably would.

Vas has attempted over the years to answer the questions posed by Mr.Hussain about what went wrong with Hindu-Muslim relations between the years of 1857 and 1947. He has, at times, thought that this question is unanswerable. "If there was an answer, we would have found it by now," he says.

Perhaps we need to dig deep into ourselves. To reason and think before we feel. To be prepared to dismiss our own cognitive and emotional biases which lead to errors in interpretation. These errors explain why problems in the realm of race relations, caste, and class have remained intransigent.

Truth and reconciliation have to come in that order. Vas reminds his friends that we cannot reconcile our differences unless we are truthful first. This means admitting our mistakes and atoning for past sins. Only then can we heal and begin anew. Anything less is a Band-Aid that peels off with the slightest wiggle.

As this novel comes to a close, the COVID crisis has exploded in India and thousands of people have died.

The world is in disarray. Even a soothsayer cannot predict what the world will look like later this month or year, leave alone the next year or the next decade. A global pandemic was not on anyone's radar. It has become the seminal event of the twenty-first century. The world will never be the same. There are challenges as well as opportunities. There is tension between unilateralism and multilateralism and between parochialism and pluralism. Whether liberal democratic forces can counter and mitigate doctrines that subvert pluralistic impulses is a burning question on everyone's mind. There are new opportunities as well. To build broader collaborations and coalitions between nations in the areas of health, trade, commerce, and culture in the post-pandemic world. Whether we will seize this opportunity or not will determine how our future will unfold.

As the gang of six from the high school class of the Sixties ponders these questions on three different continents, one question looms larger than everything else. It is this: Are we, as individuals, capable of making decisions that are rational and morally defensible?

Much depends on how we answer this call.

"Each time history repeats itself, the price goes up."[1]

---

[1] Wright, Ronald. *A Short History of Progress.* (Canongate Books, Edinburgh, 2010), 129

GLOSSARY OF INDIAN TERMS

Arey yar: Hey buddy.

Baba: An endearing term to address male children.

Bandh: A form of protest called by political activists, similar to a general strike.

Baraat: A groom brought in a procession to the marriage venue with dancing and music.

Babu: A title used in the Indian subcontinent as a sign of respect towards men.

Badam: A tree whose seeds which yield almonds which are edible and widely cultivated.

Beta: Son.

Chapati: Unleavened flat bread made of whole wheat flour.

Carnatic music: Traditional classical music associated with the south of India.

Chappal: Casual footwear usually made of leather.

Chutney: A dipping sauce made with fruits, vegetables, herbs, vinegar, sugar, and spices.

Curd: Plain yogurt.

Dada: Grandfather.

Dal: Liquid gravy vegetarian dish made with lentils and split peas.

Dhoti: A loose garment worn by males around the loins.

Diya: An oil lamp usually made of clay.

Dhokla: A soft and spongy vegetarian dish made out of gram flour and spices from the Indian state of Gujarat.

Eid: The Muslim festival of breaking the fast in the month of Ramadan.

Fanta: Orange soft drink.

Fez cap: A cylindrical felt cap usually red in colour with a tassel worn usually by Muslims.

Gandhi Cap: A white cap pointed in the front and back popularized by Gandhi during the freedom movement.

Ganesh temple: A Hindu temple dedicated to the elephant god who symbolizes wisdom. Invoked before anything new is started to bring good luck.

Ganga-Jamuni tehzeeb: The tradition that symbolizes a peaceful fusion of Hindu and Muslim cultural and religious influences.

Ghanta: A temple bell rung by devotees.

Gita: An ancient Hindu scripture which is part of the Mahabharata, dating back to the second century.

Gujarati: An Indo-Aryan language native to the state of Gujarat.

Gulab Jamun: An Indian berry sized sweet dumpling made with milk solids, sugar, rose water and cardamom.

Gulmohar: A beautiful tree that bears flowers the colour of fire. Also called a Flame Tree.

Haj (Hajj): Muslim pilgrimage to Mecca that Muslims are expected to make at least once during their lifetime.

Harijan: Meaning "Children of God," this was a term used by Gandhi for the so-called "backward classes" of India.

*HMT: H*industan Machine Tools (Indian Watch Makers)

Holi: A Hindu festival of colours heralding the arrival of spring.

IAS: Short form of Indian Administrative Service. A prestigious form of civil service.

Jalebi: An Indian sweet snack made by deep frying all-purpose flour batter. It is often soaked in sugar syrup.

Jawan: A junior soldier or infantryman of the army.

Kalamkari: Literally means "penworked." Used for creating designs with natural dyes.

Kamasutra: An ancient Indian Sanskrit text on sexuality, eroticism, and emotional fulfillment in life.

Kayasth: An educated class of people who have descended from the Kshatriyas or warrior class of the caste system.

Krishna Gana Sabha: An established association in the South that holds prestigious music and dance festivals.

Kurta: A loose collarless shirt.

Lord Venkateshwara/Balaji: A form of Hindu god who is an incarnation of Lord Vishnu, the preserver. It is the presiding deity of the Tirupati temple, which is located in the state of Telangana in South India.

Mangalsutra: A necklace that the groom ties around the bride's neck in a marriage ceremony.

Neem: A tree in the mahogany family. Grown in tropical regions. It's fruit and seeds yield a vegetable oil.

NRI: Non-Resident Indian.

Pakoda: A spiced fritter consisting of vegetables such as potatoes and onions coated in seasoned gram flour batter and deep fried.

Parsi (parsee): Members of a group of followers in India of the Persian prophet Zoroaster.

Peepal tree: A sacred fig tree native to the Indian subcontinent. Buddha is believed to have attained enlightenment under this tree.

Pitaji: Father

Pooja (puja): A worship ritual performed by Hindus to offer homage or prayer to one or more deities.

Prasad: A food offering that has been offered to the deity and then distributed to the devotees.

Puri: A deep fat fried bread made from whole wheat unleavened flour. The puffed-up, golden, brown bread is usually served with a savoury curry dish.

Rasam: A south indian spiced soup made with tamarind, tomatoes, spices and herbs.

Salam Saab: A greeting in Arabic meaning "Peace be upon you."

Salwar Kameez: Traditional combination dress. The salwar is a loose pyjama dress like trousers and kameez is a long shirt or tunic.

Sambar: A South Indian stew made with lentil, mixed vegetable, tamarind, herbs, and spices.

Scheduled Class: Demographic group officially designated as a depressed class for affirmative action.

Sepoy: An Indian soldier serving under the British or other European orders.

Sherwani: A long coat like garment originally associated with Muslim aristocracy.

Sindhoor: Traditional vermilion red mark on a woman's forehead denoting married status.

Subzi: Spicy vegetarian dish.

Tilak: A fragrant paste of sandalwood or vermillion applied on the forehead as a welcome ritual on a religious occasion.

Upma: A South Indian dish made of cream of wheat and flavoured by cooking oil, cashews, lentils, chickpeas and additional herbs and spices.

ACKNOWLEDGEMENTS

I am grateful to my wife Suhasini. But for her support and patience this would not have seen the light of day.

ABOUT THE AUTHOR

Dr. Varadaraj (Raj) Velamoor was born and raised in Hyderabad, India, a large, multi-ethnic and multi-lingual city, where he graduated from medical school in the seventies. He completed his post-graduate training in psychiatry in the United Kingdom, before moving to Canada. During his almost fifty-year career, he has practiced in different countries all over the world, including, England, Canada, the United States, New Zealand and Bermuda, and received Fellowships from professional bodies in Canada, Britain and the United States.

His approach to clinical practice, research and teaching reflect his training and life experience in a multitude of diverse cultures and health care systems, and his life long interest in examining the intersection between the biological, psychological and social realms of human behaviour. He has published over a hundred scientific papers, including book chapters and monographs, which have been widely cited and recognized in his field for clearly and cogently describing the results of his observations on a wide variety of topics. This is his first venture into writing fiction.

He lives with his wife, Suhasini, in Toronto, Canada. In his spare time, he loves to write poetry, play golf, read history and fiction, and follow current affairs.

Lightning Source UK Ltd.
Milton Keynes UK
UKHW010650070921
390173UK00002B/287

9 781039 118355